The Angel of Torremolinos

We are delighted to welcome David Serafin and Superintendent Bernal to the Macmillan list with another splendid mystery.

It is August 1982 and Bernal is still unable to disentangle himself from his increasingly empty marriage. The only solace on the horizon is his forthcoming holiday with his mistress, Consuelo, but before he can leave Madrid for the south he and all the other *comisarios* are summoned by the director to an emergency meeting. The ETA terrorists have threatened a major bombing campaign along the Spanish beaches at the height of the tourist season.

Bernal is despatched to the Costa del Sol. As he awaits the arrival of the rest of his team he discovers the local police force are worried by a number of missing foreign youths, all of whom were last heard of in Torremolinos.

The apparently motiveless murder of a detective temporarily puts the problem of the missing tourists out of his mind, but as the Superintendent deploys his staff undercover around the town the disappearances once more impinge, especially when an acquaintance of Elena and Ángel joins their number.

The puzzle of the missing tourists is one which gravely disturbs Bernal and, despite instructions from Madrid, he attempts to contain the terrorist activities while launching a full-scale investigation into the more intriguing mystery.

The outcome is a story of mounting tension as Bernal unearths an evil scheme of terror. A superb successor to David Serafin's previous novels and one that is bound to please his many fans.

THE ANGEL OF TORREMOLINOS

A Superintendent Bernal Novel

David Serafín

MACMILLAN
LONDON

First published in 1988 by
MACMILLAN LONDON LIMITED
4 Little Essex Street London WC2R 3LF
and Basingstoke

Associated companies in Auckland, Delhi, Dublin, Gaborone,
Hamburg, Harare, Hong Kong, Johannesburg, Kuala Lumpur,
Lagos, Manzini, Melbourne, Mexico City, Nairobi, New York,
Singapore and Tokyo

British Library Cataloguing in Publication Data

Serafin, David
  The angel of Torremolinos
  I. Title
  823'.914   [F]   PR6069.E61

ISBN 0–333–45820–6

Typeset by Matrix, 21 Russell St, London WC2

Printed and bound by Anchor Brendon Ltd, Tiptree, Essex

The personages and events depicted in this novel are entirely fictitious, although they are set on the Costa del Sol
in July and August 1982.

For Audrey and Matthew

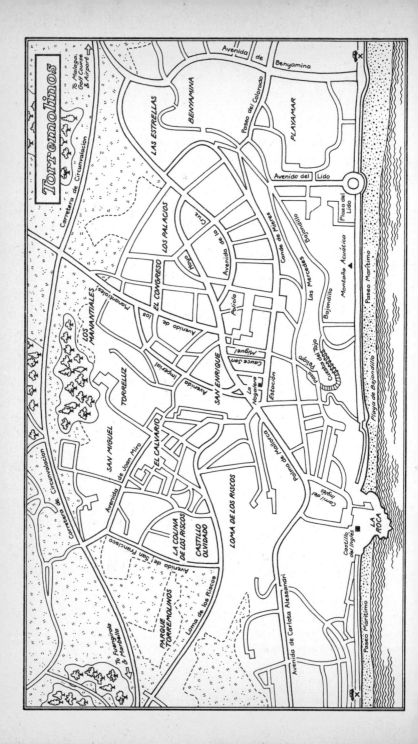

'PLEASE, PLEASE HELP ME! For Christ's sake help me!'

In surprise the middle-aged English tourist and his out-of-breath wife broke their ascent of the stone steps that zigzagged from the Bajondillo to the Calle de San Miguel in Torremolinos. They clutched each other and looked nervously up and down the gloomy lane, but could see no one.

'Come on, let's get back to the apartment,' said the pot-bellied husband. 'It's nearly four in the morning.'

'Wait,' commanded his more intrepid companion, recovering her breath. 'Someone needs help.'

She looked into the dark corner by the Britannia pub, which had already closed for the night, its chairs and tables stacked on the small triangular forecourt.

'The cry seemed to come from here.'

'There's no one there,' said her husband crossly. 'Let's get going. We shouldn't have played that fifth rubber. It cost me a thousand pesetas.'

'It was your bad bidding that cost us the rubber,' she commented indignantly.

Tiredly the stout male holidaymaker began to climb the next slope towards a bend in the steep path which was cut into the cliff-face. His buxom red-haired wife stuck her perspiring sun-reddened face over the railings that gave on to the rooftops of the Bajondillo. In the dim glow of a street-lantern fixed to the opposite wall she could make out a number of small animals moving about on the terracotta tiles in apparent alarm.

'They're cats,' she reported. 'There must be more than twenty of them.'

'*They* can't have called for help,' said her husband laconically. 'Come on, or some hoodlum will mug us and take what's left of our money.'

'But somebody cried out for help – and in English, too. Perhaps he's fallen from the wall.'

'And it could be a trap,' said her husband in a loud eerie whisper, for he had now reached the next bend in the cliff-path. 'It's one of those drug-addicts who wants money for his next fix.'

Obstinately, the woman stopped to listen for a while, watching the strangely disturbed behaviour of the cats on the darkened rooftop.

Suddenly, from above them, they could hear a clatter of feet and a kicking of empty drink-cans, accompanied by very inebriated singing.

'Come on, woman, for goodness' sake, or we'll get involved with a pack of drunks.'

She hurried to join him, and they kept to the outer side of the path as they were passed by seven burly bare-chested Swedes, who proffered apparently good-natured insults as they leap-frogged down the annoyingly wide-spaced steps of the Cuesta del Tago towards the Paseo Marítimo and the muffled sound of the breakers on the beach beyond.

The English couple now found themselves on an uninhabited section of the paved lane, where there were no bars, shops or *pensiónes* and where iron railings protected the passer-by from the precipitous cliff-edge. Once more the beer-bellied tourist stopped for breath and his inquisitive wife peered over the fence.

'I can't hear anything now,' she commented, 'but I'm sure someone's lying injured down there.'

'Forget it, will you?' gasped her overweight companion, exhausted by the climb they had made, the excessive quantity of beer he had imbibed, and the intensely humid heat which still sapped all his remaining energy even at that hour of the night. 'Let's try to get home in one piece. This town's full of foreign winos and weirdos, as well as junkies who look as though they'd slit their grandmother's throat for tuppence.'

His stout wife reluctantly left the railings and followed

him up the remaining slope, where they passed, without affording it a glance, a niche-lantern that flickered below a small statue of El Ángel de la Guarda, before which some devout person had placed a small offering of red and pink carnations.

When they turned into the small square that marked the south-eastern end of the main pedestrian street of San Miguel, which during the day formed the crammed commercial heart of Torremolinos, but which was nearly deserted at that late hour, the red-haired English woman spotted two municipal policemen who stood chatting by the small litter-filled fountain.

'I'm going to tell them about the cry we heard,' she said determinedly. 'It's our duty to inform them.'

'But you don't know enough Spanish to say "How's your father?" to them,' objected her panting husband, 'let alone explain that you think someone's fallen over the cliff. Anyway, you haven't got your phrase-book with you.'

'I'll make them understand,' she proclaimed with that imperious certainty of the English bourgeoisie, determined to be both firm and patient with half-witted foreign officialdom.

As she approached the blue-uniformed men, they hastily put out their palm-held cigarettes and saluted her gallantly.

'Somebody needs help, Officer,' she said slowly and very loudly to the senior of the two policemen, making the usual British assumption that all foreigners are stone deaf as well as childlike in their understanding. 'Down on the cliff. They must be English.' She led the officer by the sleeve and pointed across the wall opposite the restaurant installed in the remains of the tower of one of the windmills that had given the resort its name.

The municipal guard, accompanying her with extreme reluctance, looked over the edge and then back at her in puzzlement.

'You lose something, lady?' he asked in broken English.

'No, no, I haven't lost anything,' she enunciated with

extreme care. 'Somebody is lost down there.'

'Ah, not you, then?'

'No, I am here, as you can see. Someone else. A man's voice it was, speaking in English out of the darkness.' She went on in increasing desperation: 'He needs help, very urgently by the sound of it. *Now, will you go and investigate?*'

The older guard looked at the determined set of the foreign woman's jib and saluted her with great courtesy. 'Sí, sí, señora. We go investigate. You go home now.'

'Very well. So long as you go and investigate.'

'Investigate, yes, very much. We go. Now you go with your man.'

At this the woman's already reddened complexion darkened to that of the crest of a turkey-cock. 'Very well. Goodnight to you, Officer.' She took her husband's arm, and they turned into the Calle de San Miguel. ' "My man", indeed. How dare he! Anyone would think we were living in sin.'

'I don't think he meant to suggest that I was one of your occasional pick-ups, dear,' said her husband in some amusement. 'It's just that his grasp of English is only slightly stronger than yours of Spanish.'

The red-haired woman looked back suspiciously at the two municipal policemen, who were both leaning over the retaining wall lighting up fresh cigarettes. 'I don't think they're going to investigate at all.'

'Don't worry, love. You've done your civic duty by telling them about it.'

When the English couple were out of earshot, the older municipal guard commented to his companion: 'Those English women are built like battleships and fire off like them, too.' He felt his right elbow gingerly for sprains. 'She had the grip of an all-in wrestler.'

'What did she want?' asked the younger policeman, who knew even less English than his fellow.

'She lost something down on the cliff. I couldn't make out what.'

'She can come back and look for it in the daylight, whatever it is. Let's go and check out those nightclubs in the garden suburb. You know how the neighbours there complain if they don't stop the music by four a.m.'

At 8.20 a.m. on Friday, 30 July, Comisario Luis Bernal stood waiting on the platform at Norte Station in Madrid for the *electrotrén* that was due to leave for Salamanca at 8.30. He travelled as lightly as possible, with a small hand-grip that contained a change of shirt and underclothes and a spare pair of summer-weight slacks. Given his corpulence and easy propensity to perspire, he kept well out of the strong morning sunlight which had already pushed the temperature to 25° Celsius. He was glad to escape, if only temporarily, the appalling heat of the capital in midsummer, though this journey was not one he wanted to make.

Bernal had spent the previous morning in the *bufete* of a famous lawyer in the Calle de Antonio Maura, studying the possibility of filing suit for divorce from his wife Eugenia, who would surely enter a sturdy defence to prevent at all costs the dissolution of a marriage that neither partner could claim to have enjoyed. What hardened her attitude, Luis was sure, was the prospect of losing her civil status, not in Madrid where she had no social life worth speaking of, if her frequent colloquies with the narrow-minded portress were discounted, but in her native village near Ciudad Rodrigo, where she had inherited, as eldest child of her land-owning father, most of the quite unproductive hectares in the area. There she was invariably known as 'La Pétrea' – 'The Stony-Hearted' – or as 'La Comisaria', an allusion to her husband's occupation of superintendent of police.

The famous lawyer had advised Bernal to make one further attempt to persuade Eugenia to agree to a formal legal separation that could later lead to a divorce by mutual consent, and which would save him years of legal delays as well as allowing for a division of property to be properly drawn up. But Bernal

11

was not at all sanguine about his chances: he had tried to get Eugenia's consent for more than two years, though he recognised that he had made things more difficult by continuing to cohabit with her, at least in the formal sense. If he had moved out permanently to his secret apartment in the Calle de Barceló and confined himself to sending Eugenia a sufficient part of his monthly salary to cover her living expenses and the running costs of their antiquated flat off the Calle de Alcalá, then, the famous lawyer had pointed out, he would have been in a position by now to obtain a separation order at least.

Why did he continue to return to that awful dwelling day after day; to consume what he dared of her disastrous cuisine; to listen to her long rigmarole of complaints about modern society and to her extraordinary interchanges with the near-demented portress; to come back late in the evening to find Eugenia on her knees before the half-life-size statue of Our Lady of the Sorrows mounted in a cupboard off the dining-room; and then to lie down gingerly alongside her stern and chaste figure on the lumpy warped mattress uncertainly supported by the creaking bed-frame in that travesty of a matrimonial chamber? Would he never be able to break the tight bond which forty years of custom had welded, and on which, he now realised, he half-relied?

He was no good at looking after himself in any domestic matter such as washing or ironing, cooking or making beds, but he earned more than enough to pay for all these things to be done for him of course. In his secret apartment, unbeknown to his wife, all household affairs were attended to by his mistress, Consuelo, who divided her time between her work at the Banco Ibérico, looking after her invalid mother, and seeing to Bernal's sentimental and domestic needs. Being at forty-three some eighteen years younger than he, Consuelo had great energy and *joie de vivre*, only temporarily muffled, he prayed, by her shock at the stillbirth of their first, and now to be only, child. But she would spring back, he was convinced, in a month or two, when she had got over their loss and her sole adventure into motherhood. She had arranged to have the loan of her brother's duplex in the new seaside development at Puerto de Cabo Pino near Fuengirola, and wanted him to leave with her on 2 August to spend the rest of the month on the Costa del Sol, even though neither of them ever took the sun – she on account of her very fair, freckled complexion, and he through his sluggish physique and peasant-like caution over unnecessary suffering.

From his vantage-point under the soaring wrought-iron arches of the old Estación del Norte, Bernal watched the mass of trippers waiting in the intense sunlight for their trains to the Galician and Portuguese resorts. His practised eye spotted the petty criminals on the crowded platforms: feigned beggars and blind men, pickpockets and luggage-snatchers, false lottery-claimants who, by means of the trick known as the *tocomocho*, tried to convince the unwary that they had a genuine winning ticket in yesterday's draw, but for family reasons were unable to go to the Administración to collect the winnings, though they would sell it to the victim for a mere fraction of its value.

It had been his duty in his younger days to deal with such offences, which then had seemed more numerous and ingenious than today's; the economic boom of the sixties had greatly reduced mendicancy and petty confidence-tricks of this kind, but after the oil crises of the seventies there had been a new upsurge. As head of the No. 1 Homicide Group in the Criminal Brigade of the Judicial Police, his cases now involved much more serious offences, sometimes national in their importance, and, it often appeared to him, much more difficult of solution.

Bernal lit a Káiser and looked at his watch: only ten minutes late so far. Then he saw the silver and red *electrotrén* pulling into the platform. He had a first-class reservation, so didn't attempt to scramble on board among the eager holidaymakers.

In the early hours of Saturday, 31 July, the Inspector de Guardia at the National Police Comisaría in the Plaza de Andalucía sighed as he surveyed the long line of lost property

13

on the table that stretched the whole length of the guard-room. It seemed greater than the usual Friday-night haul from the bars, nightclubs and discothèques of Torremolinos.

The Inspector de Guardia groaned as he began to make out a list of more than 140 items. Most of them were books of traveller's cheques, wallets containing driving licences, national identity-cards or passports, as well as quite large quantities of money in various currencies. All of these had to be itemised against the names of the losers if ascertainable. His real headache, as usual, was with the foreigners' names, being hardly ever sure which were surnames and which fore-names, which were current addresses and which merely places of birth; the really trying ones were the Moroccan passports written in French and Arabic.

The Inspector de Guardia knew from experience that most of the lost passports and identity documents would be re-claimed by the following evening, their bearers complaining that they had been stolen from them, whereas in most cases they had merely dropped out of their pockets when their owners had had too much to drink. He never ceased to be surprised, though, by how much in the way of money and cheques was never claimed. Were the losers too scared even to enter the police station to enquire? Or did they regard their property as lost or stolen beyond redemption? He supposed that if they intended making insurance claims the companies would require a copy of the official *denuncia* of the loss before paying out. Probably they didn't even bother to insure.

The Inspector de Guardia put down his half-completed list and lit a Ducado. He picked up the telex message that had come in three hours before from Interpol and reread its staccato prose:

Have Málaga Police any information re the following persons reported missing by their relatives:

1. Jean-Paul Morillon, French citizen, civil status: bachelor, aged 19, of Besançon, profession: lorry-driver, dark brown hair and eyes, swarthy complexion, 1.82 m., 75 kilos, well built, no special marks.

14

2.   Henke Visserman, Dutch subject, civil status: bachelor (minor), aged 17, of Rotterdam, profession: stevedore, 1.58 m., 57 kilos approx., light blond hair, blue eyes; special marks: operation scar on right lower abdomen from appendix operation.

3.   Henry Albert Marks, British subject, civil status: bachelor, unemployed, aged 18, of Hackney, London, 1.75 m., 68 kilos, light brown hair, hazel eyes, blond complexion; special marks: blue tattoo on right upper arm representing heart pierced with arrow infilled with name 'Tracy' in red.

All three persons last heard of in Torremolinos between 27 June and 10 July last. Families have received no news of them since 2 July in case of Morillon, 6 July in case of Visserman and 10 July in case of Marks. Not known to be travelling together or otherwise acquainted with one another. None has criminal record in any country. Any information to Paris Central Office. Message ends.

The Inspector de Guardia groaned as he realised how long it would take him to examine the reports for the past four weeks and, worst of all, to check the enormous piles of police registration-cards required to be completed by every hotelier and *pensión* proprietor for their residents, especially since he was well aware that these were often not filled in for every guest when there was more than one in a party, and not at all by the lower sort of lodging-house keeper. If only they had access to the latest police computers in Madrid and could cross-index all the millions of records made annually at Málaga airport and along the Costa del Sol.

In any case these youths had probably drifted further along the coast towards Marbella and were sleeping rough, in which case there would certainly be no chance of finding a registration-card. Many of them were drunk the entire clock round, high on *chocolate* or other forms of marijuana or even stronger drugs smuggled in through Algeciras or Málaga and peddled, usually by Moroccans, in certain bars and discothèques. Although the Interpol message would have been transmitted to all the *comisarías* in Málaga province, the Inspector de Guardia doubted whether any would have the manpower available to examine every police report and the record-cards from every hotel and hostel along the coast, any more than he did.

In his experience, these allegedly missing youths were commonly beachcombers who would spend months or even years scrounging their way round Europe, or even further afield in Asia and India, rarely contacting their families except when they were desperate for money. They often did occasional jobs, such as washing plates in restaurants or glasses in bars, and some would turn to petty crime or to prostitution – in which case, if caught, they would be deported with an appropriate observation appended to their passport.

The Inspector de Guardia put the telex message to one side, and went on making up his list of lost property.

Superintendent Luis Bernal reached Ciudad Rodrigo at 4.40 p.m., after an annoyingly long wait at Salamanca station for the local train that eventually would go as far as the Portuguese frontier at Fuentes de Oñoro. He remembered from his earliest posting as a Civil Guard cadet in this area that this single-track railway had originally belonged to a small company which was absorbed in the late thirties by the famous Compañía del Oeste, itself in 1942 to become part of the national network, the Red Nacional de Ferrocarriles Españoles, commonly known as RENFE.

The journeys in those old trains had seemed interminable, with lengthy delays at every station for cattle to be herded aboard, goods to be loaded and passengers to be watered; at these halts the travellers could stretch limbs stiffened by the slatted wooden seats in the third-class compartments unrelieved either by corridors or lavatories. But, as the great novelist Pérez Galdós had remarked, this mode of travel was the best way to learn about one's fellow-countrymen. A typical compartment would contain: a peasant woman who managed to control two or three unruly offspring as well as a live hen tied by its legs and bundled on to the rack; a Civil Guard or serviceman resting on the butt of his rifle or submachine-gun; a shepherd or cattle-dealer wrapped in his homespun cloak with its fold to carry his provisions in; a nun with her head bent over her breviary; and a minor functionary who smoked Canary cheroots. Between them they would combine all their victuals for a picnic en route: the enormous potato and onion *tortilla* and *pistola* of bread unwrapped by the peasant woman, the shepherd's *chorizo* or blood-sausage and *bota* or leathern bottle of wine that tasted of pitch, the functionary's flat round country-loaf slit across to act as a container for thick fried slices of veal, the nun's basket of oranges and sweetmeats, and the Civil Guard's flask of *aguardiente* or cheap grape-spirit.

Nowadays this national communality and bonhomie had been largely lost, Bernal thought, by the rapid modernisation of society: the advent of the family motor-car, the constraining presence of foreign tourists on the newer trains, the essential cheapness and impersonality of travel meant that one had lost the feeling of uncertainty and adventure that the immense solitude of the Spanish landscape had once imbued in the traveller.

When the Ciudad Rodrigo taxi-driver stopped in the main square of Eugenia's village, Bernal got his bag out of the boot and fished in his wallet for the 2000 pesetas demanded, adding a tip of 200. To him it seemed outrageously expensive, for he recalled paying two pesetas fifty céntimos to make that same journey by mule-cart in the thirties, when he was courting Eugenia, even if it took a few hours longer on the unmade roads of that period.

This was Nationalist Spain's heartland, which had declared itself for Franco's uprising against the Second Republic in its early moments and which became the bread-basket of his National Movement. Even after five years of restored democracy, Bernal judged that the region had not changed its spots and was quietly biding its time until its chance would come once more.

17

Bernal banged on the ancient double-doors in the middle of the sixteenth-century façade of Eugenia's single-storey country residence. There was no reply. He tried the large handle and found the door unlocked. Inside the high-ceilinged stone-floored living-room, which still had the original curtain-screened *alcobas* or cupboard-beds on each side of the ingle-nook, he could see a stew simmering in a large iron pot on the log-fire, but there was no one in sight.

'Geñita?' he called. 'What are you up to?'

Luis noticed a pile of recently ironed baby's napkins on the scrubbed oak table and guessed that his son Santiago had already arrived with his young family for the start of the annual village fiestas and *encierros* or bullruns. He put his head round the door of the adjoining store-room and was surprised to find it fitted out as a modern bathroom in green porcelain and patterned wall-tiles. So Eugenia had given in to him to this extent. . . . Luis tried the taps in the washbasin; nothing came out. He bent to look at the pipes and found that they were not yet connected up.

How typical of Eugenia's parsimony to agree to spend nearly a million pesetas on installing a bathroom and then to deny it its function by not having it linked to the water-supply. Angrily he marched out into the large weed-covered yard, which was surrounded on three sides by long-disused stables. There was no sign of her, nor of his son and his family. Luis went through the battered gate into the overgrown kitchen-garden, where he found his daughter-in-law drawing water from the old well.

'Papá! What a surprise. We didn't think you'd come!'

Luis went over to embrace her. 'I've only come for a night. Where's my big grandson?'

'Santiago's taken him to see the bullring they're making in the church square. The baby's still asleep.' She felt something pull at the bucket in the well. 'Papá, help me with this. It's got stuck.'

Bernal bent over the sill of the well and tugged on the rope. 'We'll have to lower it and then try again.'

When he began to perspire heavily from the exertion

of lowering and then raising the heavy wooden bucket, his daughter-in-law bent to assist him. Suddenly it came up with a loud plop and deposited a large turtle at their feet.

'Oh, there's that *tortuga* again! Mamá told me it was down there. She says it's lived in the well since she was a little girl.'

'It's unhygienic,' said Bernal, eyeing the aged chelonian with extreme distaste. The latter lifted his head confidently and sniffed the evening breeze. 'Why don't you get tap-water from the neighbours across the way?'

'Mamá says this water is very clean, purer than the chlorinated stuff from the mains, but I boil it before using it for the children.'

'And the lavatory?' asked Bernal. 'Do we still have to use the straw-pile behind the orchard?'

'I'm afraid so.'

'It's scandalous,' said Bernal angrily. 'Eugenia promised to have the water-supply connected by the first of August. Where is she?'

'In the orchard picking *ratones*, or "mice" as she calls them. I think they're a kind of nectarine. She says she's going to make preserve out of them, but really they're too sour.'

Bernal wandered out through the kitchen-garden, which Eugenia had obviously been trying to weed and irrigate, and entered the large orchard, where she was nowhere to be seen. He looked about him uncertainly, until he felt a sharp blow on the nape of his neck. Glancing quickly up, he saw his wife propped high in the branches of a tree.

'Catch this basket, Luis, and pass me up that empty one.'

'How did you manage to get up there without a ladder, Geñita?'

'The usual way – like we always did – by shinning up the main trunk. I've got so many of these delicious *ratones* this year that I'm going to sell some to the neighbours.'

19

Bernal examined the basket of small, scabby, greenish nectarines and snorted: 'These are worthless, Geñita. For goodness' sake don't make another spectacle of yourself by offering them to the neighbours as though we didn't have two *cuartos* to rub together.'

'But they want these *ratones*, Luis,' she objected plaintively. 'They've offered fifty pesetas the kilo to make peach-wine, they say.'

'You're just blackmailing them as usual, Eugenia, because they know you own all their land.'

'Nonsense, Luis. Now, take that full basket and leave it in the shade in the yard. Then bring me back some more empty ones from the shed.'

'What about the mains water-supply, Eugenia? You promised to have it installed.'

'The men are coming one day this week. They are going to do it in lieu of the rent they owe me. But it's a terrible waste, all of it, Luis. You know that water comes from the artificial lake they've made alongside the Duero. It will be very dirty and full of chalk.'

'Better than having turtles in the drinking-water.'

'Rubbish! That old turtle's perfectly clean. After all, you'd eat it in a soup, wouldn't you?'

On the whole, Bernal thought, he'd rather not. He wondered how he would be able to broach again the question of divorce. Seeing Eugenia here in her natural surroundings, dressed in peasant black with her skirts tied up in country fashion to climb the fruit tree, and morally reinforced by the presence of her over-pious elder son and her innumerable relatives, he recognised that the task was well-nigh hopeless.

She would adopt her usual posture of claiming not to understand the problem. Hadn't they been married for almost forty years with all the authority of the sacraments and the law? Hadn't they procreated as Holy Scripture demanded? Hadn't she always kept herself only unto him? She would gladly draw a veil over his peccadilloes, whatever they were, and pray that he would make full confession to Father Anselmo in Madrid at the first opportunity. Repeatedly she had rehearsed her arguments: men of his age were generally known to get temporarily silly over flighty chits who only wanted to take from other, more honest, women what they had been unable to obtain for themselves. He would get over it in the end, with the Lord's help. And so the catechism would go on. Nothing would shake her, no argument would move her.

As Bernal returned with heavy step from the stable-yard with two empty baskets, he found that Eugenia had descended from the tree and was sitting under it, swigging water from a cracked earthenware *botijo*.

'This water from our well is delicious, Luisito. As good as ever it was. Here, try some.'

Bernal hoisted the dripping jar high above his head and tried to swallow a few drops. It tasted fishy.

'It's nice and cool because I stood the *botijo* in full sun and the evaporation has chilled it.'

Luis decided to take a softer tack first. 'I've made out a cheque for a million pesetas, Geñita, in your name, to pay for the bathroom.'

'Such a waste of good money, Luis, all this. My parents, and their parents before them, didn't ever feel the need for such luxuries, although they could have afforded them, so why should we indulge like this?' She tucked the cheque carefully into her apron-pocket.

'That's not the point, Geñita. You want this property to gain in value for our sons, don't you? It will be worthless if you don't modernise; they'll just demolish it after your day and sell it to the speculators, who'll build those nasty *chalés* on your land.'

She shuddered. 'They wouldn't *dare* do such a thing.'

He knew he'd got her on the raw: she loathed all the quite modest building developments that had taken place in the village on those few parcels of land that hadn't belonged to her family or herself. She would never sell any for any purpose, despite its poor agricultural quality, and she would fight for her boundaries and her water rights like a tigress whenever a dispute arose.

21

The attic-space of the house was full of dusty legal documents, and these constituted her only reading matter other than her breviary. With a large magnifying glass she would pore over the ancient legal language, muttering the phrases and place-names to herself as if they were a ritualistic reassurance of her position in the village. She had often surprised the district judge and various flashy lawyers from Salamanca with her unsurpassed knowledge of the land holdings of the whole *comarca*, and at vital moments she would produce in evidence an ancient title-deed, a copy of a contract of sale or even of a royal *fuero* going back to the thirteenth century. She always won her case, whether because the middle-aged judge was afraid of her black-garbed ramrod-straight figure with its hooked nose and its disconcerting resemblance to that of the widow of the late dictator, or because he was incapable of deciphering the imposingly authentic scrolls of parchment which she handled with such dexterity and cited aloud in Latin, Old Castilian or Leonese with great aplomb.

'That's as may be, Luis,' she went on. 'You may be right about the increased value.' This was grudgingly conceded. 'I'll see that the men connect the mains tomorrow.'

Bernal decided the time was ripe to proceed to weightier matters. 'You know I have to return to Madrid tomorrow, Eugenia. There's a lot to do in the new office building in Rafael Calvo; we still haven't arranged for our files to be put on the computer, Now, you and I must discuss again the matter of a legal separation. Will you agree to it?'

'Haven't you got that nonsense out of your head yet, Luis? A man of your age gets such absurd ideas. Instead of preparing yourself for the next world you've been turned silly by this one. Now, help me prepare the fruit for boiling. Then I'll see if the *puchero* is ready for supper.'

'But we *must* discuss it, Eugenia, or I'll have no option but to ask for the separation myself and move out of our flat in Madrid.'

'You must do what you think best, however disruptive it

will appear to everyone else. But don't count on any help from me in your foolishness.'

'And that's your last word?'

'First and last, as you well know. You want to trample on God's law. I can't and won't help you.'

In the oppressive night heat that hung over La Nogalera, in the centre of Torremolinos, Friedrich Albert lay semi-conscious under the leathery leaves of a large magnolia grandiflora, floating on a sea of beatitude. The third *porro* or reefer offered him by the Dutch girl wearing yellow shorts that revealed her long blonde legs to perfection had sent him off on a wave of incredibly sensual daydreams, in which he imagined himself being bathed, and caressed in his most intimate parts, by a bevy of Aryan blondes in a warm pool on which water-lilies floated. The sensation was so novel and previously unimaginable that he failed to perceive the delicately thieving hands searching the side-pockets of his ragged-hemmed denim shorts or the later attempt to remove his rucksack from under his head.

Most of the foreign tourists who had earlier crowded the terrace-bars that faced the small rectangular park, where they consumed enormous litre-size goblets of draught Cruzcampo beer, Coca-Cola or Fanta *de limón*, had departed now at 2 a.m. to other, indoor, pleasures, while the exhausted waiters stacked the tables and chairs for the night. The photographers, whose assistants were wont to plant live monkeys on the shoulders of prospective clients, had gone off to feed their wretched flea-covered beasts and develop their shoddy monochrome films, while the multifarious street-vendors had retired to count their takings and consume their late suppers of beefburgers smothered in patent tomato sauce.

Friedrich Albert, borne on the stupefying haze produced by the mixture of the beer he had swallowed and the canna-bis he had smoked, did not notice the small struggle under the magnolia tree or the hasty departure of the teenage thief

who had tried to remove his rucksack and who had successfully extracted his wallet and passport only to be obliged to
give them up to a smiling but powerfully built stranger.

Once alone with the unconscious blond German youth,
the tall stranger flicked open the wallet and riffled through
the nearly used-up book of traveller's cheques and the small
wad of Spanish banknotes it contained. He studied the West
German passport with care and compared the photograph
with the face of the sleeping youth. Lastly he looked at a large
key on a green plastic tag. Then he restored all the items delicately to the side-pocket of the young man's shorts, settled the
boy's head more comfortably on the salvaged rucksack, and
sat down on the raised grass verge of La Nogalera to wait.

After more than an hour had passed, Friedrich Albert began
to demonstrate the rapid eye-movements of a sleeper ex-
periencing a vivid dream, and soon his eyelids fluttered open
once or twice. Two municipal policemen strolled past on
their way to the Calle de San Miguel. The tall stranger calmly
lit a cigarette and then offered the packet to the officers.

'Is he drunk?'

'Drugged, I think. He's lodged in the Bajondillo Apartments. I'll get him down there as soon as he comes round.'

'All right. We'll leave him to you.'

The policemen lit their cigarettes and resumed their beat.
At the corner of San Miguel the younger officer looked back.
'Do you know that fellow, then?'

'Oh, yes. He's always around at this time of night. He's a
South American who runs an aid association for young people
in need – drug-addicts, runaways and the like. They call him
"The Angel of Torremolinos". He gets them back to their
digs, or finds lodgings for them, or even helps them out with
small sums if they've been robbed.'

'Seems a strange kind of occupation, especially in the
middle of the night. Is he straight?'

'We think so. He used to be a missionary, they say. One
of the few do-gooders round here. He saves *us* a lot of work,
anyhow.'

A few merry roisterers coming down from the discothèques

24

passed through La Nogalera singing drunkenly. They paid no attention to the immobile figure lying under the magnolia tree, nor to the peaceful smoker sitting near it on the grassy bed. The entrance to the underground station of the RENFE line that ran from Málaga to Fuengirola had been closed and barred some hours before; empty crisp-packets and other refuse was being borne down the escalator by the land breeze that usually blew at that hour – the *terral* as it was known – which rose so fiercely on some evenings that the passers-by had to cover their eyes to protect them from the unpleasant swirls of dust.

The *regadores* now arrived in the Nogalera square and began to connect their broad-gauge hoses to the hydrants in order to wash down the pavements and the café-terraces and to water the sparse grass and the varied shrubs and trees of La Nogalera, none of which was the walnut tree that the name of the square implied. As the *regadores* approached, letting loose powerful sprays of water, the calm seated figure of the tall stranger came to life and gently shook the shoulder of the recumbent youth.

'Hey, wake up, or you'll get a soaking!'

Friedrich Albert stirred, groaned, then tried to ungum his eyelids. He pulled himself up tentatively on to one elbow and looked up at the friendly smiling face.

'Where am I?' he asked in German.

The powerfully built stranger, who had a smattering of most European languages, told him he was in the centre of Torremolinos at four in the morning. 'Someone tried to rob you.' He saw the young man feel instinctively for the wallet in the side-pocket of his denim shorts.

'Don't worry, I stopped him and sent him packing.'

'Who are you?'

'I'm from a relief organisation for young people in trouble. I'll get you to your apartment if you like.'

A heavy jet of water hit the pavement nearest them, acting as an unspoken warning to them to get clear.

'Come on. The *regadores* will soak us if we don't move from here.' He was well aware that they would do no such thing, being extremely adept at avoiding pedestrians and motorists alike. He helped the young man to his feet and allowed him to sway uncertainly on the grass verge.

'Look, I'll carry your rucksack. Where are your lodgings?'

The young German scratched his blond head in some puzzlement and pointed to the Calle de San Miguel. 'I think it's that way. Down by the sea.'

The tall stranger took him firmly by the arm and led him on to the narrow pavement. 'Take it easy, now. Don't rush it. Did you drink a lot of beer?'

'A few *Steinen*, yes. But a Dutch girl gave me some grass to smoke. That's the last I can remember.'

'Well, don't worry. I don't think you've lost anything, and by tomorrow you'll feel much better.'

With infinite patience he led the young tourist down the Calle de San Miguel past the darkened and shuttered shops and cafés, round the small fountain near the Windmill restaurant, down the long series of widely spaced steps of the Cuesta del Tago towards the Paseo Marítimo. The heady scent of the white-flowered summer jasmine enveloped them as they passed under the niche sheltering the statuette of the Guardian Angel.

The young German staggered slightly from time to time; he was glad of the strong arm that supported him and was thankful he did not have to carry his rucksack.

'Do you remember the name of the place you are staying in?'

'I'd only just booked in there. I spent all the afternoon looking for a place. It's near the Lido Square. A kind of garden surrounded by two storeys of chalets. I had to come back up here to the tourist office for my luggage.'

'I know it, I think.'

They turned out of sight of the lamp burning under the statue on to a dark stretch of the steep path cut into the cliff-face. The railings that stood between them and the long drop to the rooftops of the Bajondillo served for a while as a resting-place for them both. The tall stranger lit up a Winston and offered one to the German youth.

26

'Danke. I don't smoke.'

The powerfully built stranger smiled, and laughed inwardly. The boy didn't smoke, but he smoked pot.

Below them from the pantiles of the roofs there came a sudden howling almost like that of a human infant. It startled the German youth.

'Was ist das?'

'Just my cats having a squabble, I expect.'

'Your cats?'

'I call them "my cats" but they're really strays. Some of them are wild. You should see them spit and fight. They are mine only because I feed them, you see.' He smiled disarmingly. 'Let's get you home now. You could do with some sleep.'

'You can say that again.' The blond German smiled gratefully at the reassuring stranger and grasped his arm in a gesture of camaraderie. 'Let's get going!'

As he touched his arm, he did not see the sharp twinge on the face of his companion, nor did he notice the sudden stiffening of his arm muscles. Later, without knowing how he had got there, Friedrich Albert found himself completely relaxed on a very soft double-bed in a room lined with apricot-silk draperies and adorned with large vases of gladioli spikes. He dreamt he was once more in the pool full of water-lilies, being attended by the blonde houris, only now he was appalled to see they were turning into ravenous, mange-ridden, flea-infested wild-cats.

Only later, much later, would come the strangely inhuman indignities, the traumatic horror, the blood blinding his eyes, the tearing, searing pain, and then the blackness.

Superintendent Luis Bernal returned to Madrid on Saturday, 31 July in a black temper. It was true that he had got in earlier than he had hoped by making a good connection at Salamanca with an Irún-bound express that took him to Medina del Campo, where he had just caught the Europa

27

express for Madrid-Chamartín. Since it was only 5.45 p.m. he decided to take a taxi straight to the new Policía Nacional building in the Calle de Rafael Calvo to see how his second-in-command, Inspector Francisco Navarro, was coping with the move from the old building in the Puerta del Sol.

Not that Bernal had any worries on that score: Paco was the most efficient inspector in the Criminal Brigade, adept at filing and paperwork. He hadn't worked outside the office for more than twenty years, except in emergencies, being naturally shy with people and a desk-man by inclination. In the five days since all their paraphernalia had been transported from the battered and overcrowded office-space in the Calle de Correo, Paco would have put everything into some sort of order and requisitioned the filing-cabinets and other furniture they needed.

It was stiflingly hot in the taxi that took Bernal down La Castellana from the shiny new railway station at Chamartín, and the city looked even more deserted than when he had left it the day before. These were the crucial days of Operación Salida when more than a million and a half *madrileños* departed for the coast or the sierra, leaving the *paseos*, boulevards and *rondas* almost empty of traffic and the street cafés half-deserted. The only people who would remain in the capital were those too poor to go on holiday, the workers who had been unlucky enough to draw July or September for their annual break, and those *Rodríguez* or grass-widowers who had deposited their wives and children in mountain *chalés* or seaside apartments and in their absence were looking forward to living it up in whatever was left of the capital's nightlife.

The taxi drew up outside the gleaming building of concrete and copper-coloured glass, and Bernal paid off the driver. He fished in his pocket for his newly issued special pass and presented it to the bored-looking brown-and-beige-uniformed guards at the entrance. They saluted and let him through the electrically controlled doors.

Bernal felt lost in the vast marble-lined hall and looked round for the lifts to go up to the sixth floor. There he found

Inspector Navarro fixing an aluminium sign to the outer door of their impersonal office-suite: *Homicide Group No. 1: Superintendent L. Bernal*.

'That's very smart, Paco.'

'It's just come from the workshops, Chief.' Navarro wiped his hand with his handkerchief and shook hands with his superior. 'Wait till you see the computer terminal they've given us. I don't think I'll ever master it, *jefe*.' He ushered Bernal into his personal office.

'Have the others all gone on holiday, Paco?' Bernal guessed that his elegant female inspector, Elena Fernández, would have left with her parents for their seaside mansion at Sotogrande, while his youngest and wildest inspector, Ángel Gallardo, would probably be on his way to Benidorm or some similar resort with one or two of his many girlfriends to whoop it up for a fortnight.

'Elena went yesterday, Chief, and I expect the others are about to leave, though I'm not sure that Lista and Miranda are going further than the Sierra de Guadarrama with their families.'

One of the phones rang in the outer office, and Navarro went to try to work out which one of them it was.

'I'm not used to these yet, *jefe*. It must be the internal one.' He picked up the receiver and listened for a moment. 'It's for you, Chief.' He placed the palm of his hand over the mouthpiece. 'It's the Director's secretary. They want you for an urgent meeting of the *comisarios* in half an hour's time. Shall I say you're out of town?'

Bernal sighed and took the instrument from him. 'I'd better take it and see what's up.'

The office of the Director of the Security of the State was still in the Gobernación building in the Puerta del Sol, in the old heart of Madrid. This imposing structure, surmounted by a Normal Clock, the tinny chimes of which were familiar to every Spaniard from the news bulletins on Radio Nacional, had originally been built as the main post office, until that had been moved in the twenties to the new 'wedding-cake' structure, jocularly known as 'Our Lady of the Communications', in the Plaza de Cibeles. The older pink-and-white pile had much earlier passed to the Ministry of the Interior, popularly called the Gobernación.

Bernal got out of the official car that Navarro had ordered for him and showed his gold-star badge to the four national policemen under the main portico. He wondered how many of his fellows of equal rank would turn up on the evening before the August holiday, when traditionally all the ministries wound down to a caretaking pace until the third week in September. It seemed to him only yesterday that Franco's top civil servants used to follow the old monarchist tradition and move lock, stock and barrel to San Sebastián from 19 July to 'El día de las Mercedes – the Day of Mercies – on 24 September while the Caudillo spent his summer entertaining guests on board his yacht *Azor* and sailing to and fro between El Ferrol and the summer capital. The restored Bourbon monarch and his family preferred a shorter, more active participation in summer sports and moved to the Marivent Palace in Palma, where King Juan Carlos took part in yacht races. Nowadays the civil servants, or some of them at least, had to stay in the heat of the capital while the ministers flew to Majorca for occasional audiences with the King.

As soon as he entered the Gobernación, Bernal's highly developed nose picked up the scent of trouble and his eyes spotted an unusual bustle of activity. There was some sort of flap on, he was certain. In any case, whoever remembered a meeting of all the *comisarios* being called at short notice, except when the Vice-President had been assassinated in December 1973?

At the top of the gilt-railed staircase he was met by his old enemy, the Sub-Secretary, who looked flushed with anxiety.

'Thank Heaven you hadn't left the city, Bernal. I'm afraid that a lot of your colleagues have gone and we've had to send urgent messages of recall.'

'What has happened, Mr Secretary?'

'The Director will explain when you're gathered. It's all top-secret.'

In the large council chamber overlooking the Puerta del Sol, Bernal found a number of his fellow-superintendents, including Zurdo, whom he greeted warmly and congratulated on his recent promotion to *subcomisario* with headship of his own homicide group.

'What's it all about, Zurdo?'

'Something to do with ETA, I've heard, the military branch. A new threat to security, the desk sergeant says.'

'Well, he always knows more than the Director. It's not another ETA commando in the capital?'

'It must be more than that, Chief, because they've re-called the heads of all the groups, including Anti-Vice and Drugs.'

A hush fell over the room as the Director entered accompanied by the Sub-Secretary and the Chief Superintendent of the new Anti-Terrorist Section. The short but imposing Director stood at the head of the table before the scanty group of fifteen superintendents and asked them to be seated. The Sub-Secretary meanwhile came along the conference-table importantly handing out sealed blue-covered files.

'Gentlemen, it seems that many of your colleagues have already gone on leave.' A slight titter broke out and was quickly suppressed. 'Don't worry, they are being recalled for special duty like the rest of you.'

The Director turned to the wall behind him to lower a projection-screen and asked for the window-blinds to be pulled down. One of his aides switched on a projector, and the lights were dimmed.

'You can see on the screen an enlargement of the communication the Information Section has received this morning from ETA *militar*. We have ascertained that it is genuine and not a hoax by checking with the agreed codes.'

Bernal had always thought it extraordinary that legally elected governments should pre-arrange identification-codes with terrorist organisations of any hue, but he knew that it was worldwide practice nowadays.

'You will see that the letter demands the immediate withdrawal of the National Police, the Civil Guard and the

31

armed forces from the three Basque provinces plus Navarre, and the creation forthwith of an independent Basque state on both sides of the Pyrenees.' There were a few gasps from his audience, but Bernal remained silent at Zurdo's side. 'An emergency meeting of ministers was held at midday today, and the President has flown to Palma to consult with His Majesty the King. I have to inform you that the Council's decision is irrevocable: there is no possibility of giving in to any of these demands.' There was a strong murmur of approbation. 'ETA gives the Government seventy-two hours to begin implementing its proposals; after that it will proceed to explode bombs at all the chief tourist resorts without any prior warning.'

There was an outburst of angry comments from the *comisarios*. The Director held up his arm for silence. 'The Minister of the Interior has instructed me to take every available measure to foil these threats. In addition, the Minister of Defence has asked the JUJEM to place the army bomb-disposal squads on stand-by and our Ministry has put the GEOs or Special Operations Groups on full alert. It is clear to us that the provincial police forces and the Civil Guard do not at present possess the necessary manpower or resources to cope with a threat of this magnitude, especially as they are already policing some forty million tourists, taken over the summer season as a whole.'

The Director asked for the lights to be put on and pulled down a large-scale political map of the Peninsula. 'To give just one example: the Málaga force, which normally serves just under half a million inhabitants, finds itself during the summer policing nearly five million people, most of whom are from Northern Europe and hardly speak a word of our language. Now, you can see from the map where the main tourist centres are and how they are dotted along the coastal provinces in various military regions: the north coast from San Sebastián through Santander and Gijón to Galicia, where the main body of holidaymakers are nationals or French.' He paused for a moment. 'In the files in front of you, you will find some facts and figures from the Ministry of Information

32

and Tourism about the usual pattern of summer tourism. It seems to me that there is little risk of explosions in Guipúzcoa itself, since even dogs don't usually foul their own kennels.' There was again a titter from some of the audience. 'Apart, that is, from their usual shooting matches and setting fire to French vehicles.'

He picked up a long wooden pointer and indicated the eastern and southern coasts. 'Our biggest problem clearly lies here, along the *Costas*, from the Costa Brava to the Costa Cálida at Cartagena, and then from Almería through Málaga and the Costa del Sol as far as Sotogrande. There is a much smaller risk to the coast along the Estrecho to Cadiz and the mouth of the Guadalquivir. The number-one targets must be Callela de Palafrugell, Lloret and Tossa de Mar, Calpe, Benidorm, Alicante, La Manga, Nerja, Torremolinos, Fuengirola, Marbella and Estepona, since they have the highest number of tourists.' He turned again to the map. 'Now, as you can see, a large number of provincial police forces are involved in the operation we are going to mount. We shall call it "Operación Guardacostas". The immediate aim is to reinforce plain-clothes supervision of these main resorts, plus some of the lesser ones, with all the groups we can spare from the inland cities where the population has been more than halved because of the summer exodus. But this secondment must be carried out in the utmost secrecy; it wouldn't do for our local villains to get the idea that they're being left a clear field for the rest of the summer.' There was another nervous titter from his small audience. 'Now the Chief Superintendent of the new Mando Único Antiterrorista, who is known to most of you, will explain in detail what the duties of your groups are to be, and then the Sub-Secretary will give you your allocations.'

Bernal looked with curiosity at the head of this new force, which was really only a revamping of the old Information Section. He remembered this high-ranker as a pushy young inspector in the Socio-Political Police during the immediate aftermath of the Civil War; then he had been hell-bent on rooting out anyone with the faintest liberal tendencies and

33

sending them to 'rehabilitation camps' or straight to the execution squads, depending on the relative gravity of their support for the ill-fated Second Republic. As this Chief Superintendent, who must by now be in his late sixties and past the official retiring age, rose to address the gathering, Bernal glimpsed the hard burning eyes and thin-lipped yet sensual mouth he had once seen in a Berruguete portrait of Torquemada. How often these steely bigoted types recurred in the unhappy governance of Spain, thought Bernal. Was it extreme religious fervour that drove them, or sheer hatred of their fellow-men?

Bernal sensed that all his companions who had turned like him towards this red-faced pot-bellied scourge, once of communists and Freemasons, and now of terrorists, were scared of him, since none of them dared look him in the eye as Bernal was now boldly doing.

The Chief Superintendent sensed Bernal's calm scrutiny of his fleshy over-indulged features, and tried to outstare him, just as he had done in the days when they were rounding up the members of the *checas* in Madrid in April and May 1939. Bernal withstood the ocular ferocity of his old secret opponent that bored into him almost like that of a stoat trying to fascinate a rabbit. So taken was he with the man's close likeness to the Torquemada portrait that Bernal found himself unable to avert his gaze even had he wanted.

The power of these inquisitors was quickly waning, for even the present nervously right-of-centre Government felt strong enough to ditch such tyrannical figures at the first sign of failure in their repression of regional terrorism. All the activities of the forces of law and order were now much more open to criticism in the press, especially in *El País* and *Cambio 16*, and even the partially reformed judiciary was acquiring a new spirit of independence and was beginning to throw its weight about.

Bernal felt in tune with the new epoch that was opening; this figure belonged to forty years of Francoist repression, and the days of his continued exercise of naked and unaccountable power were surely numbered.

After an awkward pause, during which his colleagues coughed nervously, fumbled with their blue files, or lit up cigarettes, the Chief Superintendent broke off his attempt to make Bernal pay the small act of obeisance of being the first to lower his eyes, and waved to the projectionist to put up a series of police photographs. Childishly Bernal felt he had won a tiny victory, but he wondered how dear it would cost him later on.

'Gentlemen, these are the mugshots my group has obtained of the members of ETA *militar* we most want to capture.'

As the lights were dimmed once more, the assembled superintendents looked hard at the stark monochrome slides. Of these Basque terrorists (or freedom-fighters, depending on one's political standpoint, Bernal thought wrily), most appeared on the screen in a number of disguises: sometimes clean-shaven and short-haired in shots obviously taken some years before; sometimes, in secretly and more recently acquired snaps, wearing beards and moustaches with longer or even dyed hair. Below each set of photographs were the name and aliases, including the Basque military nickname.

'All these terrorists have been arrested in previous sweeps,' the Chief Superintendent went on, 'but the Government in its supreme wisdom' – this was uttered with heavy and pejorative irony – 'has let them loose to roam again on the streets of our cities or has allowed them to slip across the frontier into France. It will seem incredible to you, I know, but we are fighting this mini-civil war with both hands tied behind our back.'

The Director of State Security began to look uncomfortable, Bernal could see in the reflected glare of the now empty screen.

'Now,' continued the head of the Anti-Terrorist Unit, 'the entire resources of the State are to be unleashed on a gang of fifty or sixty brigands who hold their fellow-citizens to ransom, as they did a few months ago with the father of the singer Julio Iglesias, and who extort protection money, or "political tax" as they call it, from businessmen in order to acquire arms and explosives with which to murder our army officers, soldiers, policemen and Civil Guards. Our task must be to sweep them off the face of Spain and return to the forty years of peaceful coexistence!'

As the Chief Superintendent's voice rose in a fanatical cry, the Director once more exhibited signs of unease, but he did not dare to intervene.

'These criminals rob our banks of large sums to buy arms from abroad, they steal explosives from our quarries, and they make interchanges with foreign terrorists. The armoury belonging to ETA *Político-militar*, which I was influential in capturing in February of this year, contained a vast arsenal – enough to keep a minor war going for three months. Thank God that's not available to them now, at any rate. We've got them on the run!'

Some run, thought Bernal, if the reformed ETA *Militar* was able to carry out its threats to the entire tourist trade so vital to the country's balance of payments.

'We must find these men, especially those eight whose mugshots I have shown you, copies of which you will find in your files, together with the two women who are as bloodthirsty and as cut-throat as their menfolk.' The Chief Superintendent now invited them to study the outline of Operación Guardacostas as set out in their files. 'The task of your respective groups, once you have been allocated to a particular resort, will be to search out these ETA commandos; not just by *búsqueda y captura* – "find and arrest" – but shooting to kill on sight. Don't take any more chances with them than you would with rabid dogs!'

The anti-terrorist chief now asked for the blinds to be raised and he turned to the wall-map. Bernal noticed that he didn't seek to make further eye-contact with him. He seemed drunk, not with alcohol, but with power.

He took up a long wooden pointer. 'The bomb-disposal squads and GEOs are being quartered in key positions: Tarragona, Cartagena, Seville, Jerez, Santiago de Compostela and Santander. There are already sufficient permanent squads of them in the Basque country. The Barcelona police will handle the Catalan coast and the Balearic islands. As it happens, there is tight security by land, sea and air in Majorca throughout August because of the Head of State's temporary residence there.'

Bernal noticed he didn't refer to the King and the royal family directly; for this dinosaur it was as though the Movimiento Nacional still existed in all its manifestations and with its original organic and vertical structures.

'The Head of Security in Catalonia is in direct contact with me at all times, in case reinforcements become necessary. The Madrid groups will be employed principally to strengthen the south-eastern and southern resorts where the main threat lies, and to a lesser extent the northern ones. Under the direction of my Mando Unico, you will have powers to override the local authorities and take any action you think fit to prevent any bombings and eliminate these killers. If any incidents occur, you are to report them to me immediately for assessment, but shoot first and tell me about it afterwards!'

Again Bernal had the impression that this was a bit too much for the Director of State Security, who now intervened. 'The Chief Superintendent and I expect to have minute-by-minute reports if there is any incident, and we shall issue any necessary orders and send in reinforcements as required. There is to be a complete clamp-down on publicity: no statements are to be made to the press, radio or television about Operación Guardacostas, is that understood?'

Bernal dared to ask a question. 'If there is an explosion, how shall we be able to stop it being reported by all who hear it?'

'The Minister of the Interior will handle the matter, Comisario,' said the Director. 'The emergency provisions will be invoked and a restriction notice issued to the editors and agencies concerned.'

'And the foreign pressmen, how will you stop them publishing it?'

'That's a question for the Minister for External Affairs.'

Bernal couldn't see how anyone could prevent it, unless they censored despatches and tapped all the telephones – an impossible task with international dialling available in every kiosk and millions of tourists ringing home every day. They could hardly hold them all incommunicado. It was clear that the ministers hadn't thought the matter through, but he didn't persist.

When the meeting ended, Bernal looked at Zurdo quizzically. 'Do you understand how we are to suppress news of any explosions?'

'No, Chief, it's beyond me. The international correspondents will be on it in a flash, and the foreign radio broadcasts and newspapers will carry it immediately.'

'Exactly, and it is precisely in the seaside resorts where most of the imported newspapers are sold.'

They had to queue in front of the Sub-Secretary's desk to find out where they were to be seconded. When it was Bernal's turn, the politically appointed official, with whom he had never got on well, looked up with some glee: 'Your group is allocated to the Málaga section, Comisario. The Chief Superintendent of Anti-Terrorism has especially asked for you to be sent to Torremolinos, given your record and experience and the fact that it is a certain target. The Director wants your group to be in Málaga by Monday evening at the latest. The ultimatum expires at midday on the third of the month.'

Bernal made no comment. Although, because of Consuelo's holiday plans, Marbella or Fuengirola would have been more convenient, his posting could have been much worse – at Gijón or Santander for instance. He waited for Zurdo and found that as luck would have it he was being sent to Fuengirola.

'At least I'll have a friend within shouting distance, Zurdo. In any case I'd planned to spend a fortnight's holiday staying near your patch.'

'That's great, Chief. We'll meet in Málaga Monday evening, then.'

Before leaving the Gobernación, Bernal rang Navarro at their new office and explained about their recall and special assignment. 'Can you get messages to all the others to make their way to the Gobierno Civil building in Málaga in order to arrive there by seven p.m. tomorrow? You'd better book all the accommodation you can for the group in Torremolinos. Enlist the help of the local National Police if necessary, but tell them to be discreet. This is meant to be an undercover operation.'

Coming out into the intense heat of the Puerta del Sol, with the harsh voices of gypsy women selling lottery tickets raised against the rumble of the evening traffic, Bernal was almost tempted to stop at the corner of Carretas and buy a glass of *horchata de chufas* – that refreshing milk of crushed tiger-nuts – but perhaps it wouldn't do if the Director were to catch sight of him imbibing in the street. He took Line 1 of the Metro to Tribunal and there emerged into the shady gardens in front of the Barceló theatre. Denying himself his usual apéritif of a Larios *gin-tónic* in the large cafeteria near his secret apartment, he went straight up to break the news to Consuelo, who would surely be packing for the journey.

As he let himself into the apartment, he could hear Bizet's L'Arlésienne Suite being played loudly on the Hitachi hi-fi system, and Consuelo came dancing out of the lounge in a pale blue négligé to greet him. Luis thought he hadn't seen her look so happy for months, certainly not since the traumatic experiences she had recently endured in Las Palmas which caused her to miscarry and her – their – daughter to be stillborn.

'Isn't it fabulous, Luchi?' She threw herself at him, making him fall into an armchair, and then kissed him passionately. 'My brother's going to drive us down to Cabo Pino in his Mercedes after all. He had to come back last Friday on business and now he has to go back to collect my sister-in-law and their children who have been there since mid-July. He says there'll be less of a *caravana* tomorrow, since most holidaymakers will have travelled yesterday or today.'

'How will you manage for a car when you're there, Chelo?'

'We'll hire one for a fortnight on the spot. You know how I hate driving long distances.'

'Who's going to look after your mother?'

'Oh, I've engaged an additional nurse for ten days until my sister-in-law gets back. You know Mamá hardly recognises me any more, so it shouldn't worry her.'

Bernal wondered how to break the news about Eugenia's intransigent attitude towards the question of a legal separation. He thought he'd better leave the matter until they were more relaxed at Cabo Pino unless Consuelo asked about it.

'I'd better tell you right off that there's a flap on in the Ministry, Chelo, and I've been put on special duty from Monday.'

Her face fell, and she looked as though she would cry. 'Oh, no, they always manage to ruin our holiday plans!'

'It's not as bad as that. My group is being sent to Torremolinos for the month, which is only thirty kilometres along the coast. Navarro is booking us hotel rooms, but I thought I'd try to come home to you each evening unless things get tough.'

'What's it all about, Luchi?'

'It's top-secret, but ETA is involved.'

'I thought things had been very quiet since the spring. I suppose you'll be leaving me high and dry all day long.'

'Perhaps you'll meet a young Scandinavian on the beach and have a summer fling.'

She slapped him playfully. 'Now, you know I only like older men with experience. The young ones don't appeal to me at all.'

On the evening of Sunday, 1 August, Inspector Ángel Gallardo was sitting on a high stool at the bar of a small hotel in Benidorm having a tiff with Mercedes, the longest-lasting and most faithful of his many girlfriends.

'Why did you agree to come, Merche, if you're going to be jealous and bad-tempered all the time?'

'It's not fair, Ángel, you're always the same with your roving eye. The way that Swedish girl behaved on the beach was scandalous. Apart from prancing about nearly nude in

40

that ugly monokini, she was deliberately throwing the beach-ball at you so that she could stand over you to reach for it.' Ángel rolled his eyes lasciviously. 'That's just it,' she went on angrily. 'You were encouraging her.'

'Well, when you're offered it on a plate, you've got to make a grab for it, haven't you?'

She slapped him quite hard on the cheek and burst into tears. 'You're insufferable! I'm going up to the room to lie down.'

'Without me?' he called after her. But she flounced out into the hall without looking round.

Ángel sat ruefully rubbing his face and asked the sympathetic barman for another *caña* of Cruzcampo beer. It had been a mistake to bring her; he realised that even after only twenty-four hours. When he travelled with two girlfriends it usually worked out much better, since they would vie for his attentions at first and only later would they gang up on him. Mercedes was clearly more prickly than usual. Perhaps it was her age: at twenty-four she was probably afraid of getting left on the shelf. In fact she'd always seemed to be the one he felt he could marry if it weren't for her extremely jealous nature. He could hardly look at another girl in her presence without the storm warnings being hoisted, and in a place like this, loaded with eager blonde foreigners, how could he not take a look at any rate? What harm did it do? It was inhuman of her to expect him to lower his eyes as though he were a monk.

Suddenly a deeply tanned elbow nudged him. 'Buy me a drink?'

It was the Swedish girl from the beach, now sporting a stunning blue après-swim outfit.

'What you like?' he asked in broken English.

'Me? Everything you like. I all-rounder.'

Ángel looked nervously at the door to the hallway, hoping Mercedes hadn't got over her fit of pique and taken it into her head to make a sudden reappearance.

'Why don't I take you to a quiet club I know?' he said in Spanish.

'A club? Why not?'

'Ah, you know it, then. That's what it's called: Why-Not?'

It was getting dark as Ángel and the bosomy Swede, whose name he found so strange he could neither pronounce it nor imagine it written down, returned arm-in-arm along the palm-fronded promenade below the old church of Benidorm.

'Your girl, she very jealous?' The idea obviously gave her great satisfaction.

You can say that again! thought Ángel, looking surreptitiously at his wristwatch. It was 9.45 and the crowds taking the evening *paseo* were thinning as dinner-time approached.

'Much jealous!' He made a sign of cutting his throat with his finger.

The Swedish girl giggled and wriggled her hips. 'I good competition for her, then.'

If she doesn't stab you to death on the spot, Ángel thought. As they reached the end of the promenade, which was ill-lit and deserted, Ángel could see a figure bending over a spade at the edge of the beach under the sea-wall.

'I wonder what he's up to.'

The girl followed the direction of his gaze and laughed. 'Fish, shellfish he look for.'

Nearby in the shadows Ángel saw a red-haired woman standing by a car, looking anxiously up and down the promenade and then back at the man who was digging. As Ángel and the blonde girl passed, the woman fished a cigarette out of her handbag and lit it nervously. When he and the girl began to ascend the slope that led towards the old church, Ángel looked back in curiosity. In the reflected light from the shops and bars opposite, he could see the man filling in the hole and gently smoothing the surface of the sand. Then he and the woman hurried to a small yellow Citroën parked under the palm trees and drove off along the esplanade.

Ángel's policeman's instincts were mildly aroused. What a strange thing. What had they been up to? Ah well, he shrugged, the hole had been too small to bury a body in.

Back at the hotel lobby, he parted tenderly from the over-friendly Swede, who told him her room number, and then turned to come face to face with Mercedes' coldly furious and tear-stained face.

'Here, this urgent message was brought by the local police for you. You'd better read it.'

She turned abruptly and stalked off towards the dining-room without giving him a backward glance.

At Sotogrande on the night of 1 August, Inspectora Elena Fernández found herself already overcome by boredom on the second day of her holiday. Her rich parents were kind, too kind, in that they cocooned her from all manifestations of normal existence.

The main interest of her father in Sotogrande lay in the numerous *chalés* he was building there. Having amassed considerable wealth in the high-rise building boom in Madrid during the sixties and early seventies, in recent years he had turned to this small but elegant fishing-port north-east of Gibraltar where he was well on the way to doubling his earlier fortune. He had reserved the best and most seclud-ed site near the Torre de Guadiaro for his own mansion, which had private access to the beach – although even he, much to his chagrin, couldn't prevent vulgar holidaymakers from invading what he regarded as his territory, since the fifteen-metre strip above high-water everywhere belonged to the Patrimonio Nacional and was therefore for the use of all citizens.

After dinner this evening Señora de Fernández had dis-missed the servants and asked Elena to accompany her to the local five-star hotel, at which juncture her father announced he was off to the golf club to meet his business partners.

'We'll have a coffee there, Elena dear,' her mother cooed. 'Such a nice class of person one finds in the Palm Lounge, and perhaps a good-looking rich young man for you. Then we'll have a little flutter if you like.'

She knew very well that her mother's only real passion nowadays was for playing bingo, and she simply wanted an excuse to get to the hotel. Elena's spirits sank as she realised she was in for thirty more nights like this one. Why couldn't she summon up the courage to make the break from this annual torture, and tell her father that she was going off to Portugal with a boyfriend?

Not that she had had many boyfriends; in her undergraduate years at the Complutense she had had a series of mildly innocent affairs and at the Escuela Superior de Policía she had formed a more serious attachment with an older man. But this had cooled – mainly through her mother's interference, she considered. Being an only child of rich parents she was in a peculiarly difficult situation. They had been appalled when she had grasped the opportunity to enter the Police School as one of the first of the female graduate entrants and they were horrified when she had passed out top of her year and then been made an inspector.

Elena had been proud to become attached to Superintendent Bernal's Homicide Group in the Criminal Brigade: a lot of eyebrows had been raised at the DGS, as it then was, by her appointment and Bernal's acceptance of it. But she had made a success of the posting, and Bernal had become more of a father to her than her own flesh and blood. Her chief treated her as a professional, and she knew she fitted usefully into his team.

Over the past five years she had become remote from her parents' social circle, and they were becoming resentful of the fact. They wanted her to 'marry well' and provide them with grandchildren to inherit their wealth; although she never spoke out on the matter, she felt that they should have covered their bets by having more offspring than her. Elena was ever more fascinated by police work and knew that she wouldn't give up her independence for anyone.

After an hour and eight games of utter boredom, she noticed that her mother had settled down with two haute-bourgeoise ladies who were also on holiday from Madrid, and the three of them were obviously bent on making it a long night of gossip and gambling.

'Mamá, I have a headache coming on. I think I'll go home to bed.'

'Very well, dear. Take the car if you like. I'll call a taxi when I'm ready to come.'

'Don't dream of it, señora. We'll take you home of course.'

'How very kind. Here are the keys, Elena.'

'I'd rather walk, really. It's only three hundred metres. Perhaps the cool air will clear my head.'

'Be very careful, then, my dear. So very unsafe nowadays, with muggers and rapists behind every bush. Are you sure you'll be all right?'

'I'm sure.' Elena tapped her handbag. 'After all, I've got my pistol.'

The other two ladies were shocked, and Señora de Fernández looked at Elena reprovingly.

'My daughter's a police inspector, you know, in the Brigada Criminal. My husband and I were against it, but young people nowadays, what can you do? Of course we are hoping that she'll soon be promoted to *comisario*—'

Elena escaped from the smoky lounge and emerged on to the palm-lined road. The residual heat of the day and the heavy scent of the large-flowered jasmine enveloped her like a perfumed silken robe, and she felt she really would get a headache. She gained the fresher air of the beach road where there was little street-lighting and she glimpsed the opalescence of the waves breaking gently on the shingle under the dim light of the new moon. Perhaps she ought to observe the old gypsy superstition and turn a silver coin towards it for luck.

There was no one in sight on the narrow promenade, and the sound of the bingo numbers being called and the sentimental music from the Palm Lounge receded, until she could hear only the loud rasping of the cicadas in the low shrubs beyond the roadway and the moaning of the breakers. Ahead Elena could see the lights of her father's mansion set in a lamp-lit garden on the height at the end of the bay.

All at once she heard a thud on the steps of the promenade in front of her and she stopped in surprise and held on to the railings to look over on to the beach. She could make out only the sunshades made of dried palm-fronds and occasional tarpaulin-covered piles of deck-chairs. She listened for a while but heard nothing more. Perhaps the light breeze had blown a chair over.

Elena strolled on more slowly, glancing at the darkened beach from time to time. She was now approaching one of the flights of steps that led down from the promenade. Suddenly she heard another, louder, thud and a muffled curse. She stopped again and clutched her handbag, reassured by the bulk of her small service revolver. She peeped cautiously over the edge and thought she could see two dark figures under one of the sunshades. Listening intently, she waited. It could be that they were just a courting couple who were taking a midnight bathe – it was certainly warm enough – or merely seeking a quiet place to make love. The dark figures she had glimpsed seemed to merge into the heavy shadows and disappear.

Elena walked slowly on, making no noise in her light Gucci moccasins as she passed the top of the flight of stairs. Soon she reached the steep path that led to her father's house, where she paused to unlock the wrought-iron gates. Turning to shut them again, she saw two figures climbing up the steps from the beach to the road where they got into a car parked opposite. Just a pair of lovers, as she had supposed, though she was puzzled by the man's carrying what appeared to be a spade or similar implement, which he placed in the boot before driving off at speed. Could they have been digging up mussels? She had never heard that there were any at Sotogrande.

As she approached the front door, she heard the phone start to ring and she hurried in to answer it.

'Paco? Paco Navarro! How wonderful to hear from you. Where's the Chief?'

46

She listened with growing delight as she heard of her recall to special duties and she couldn't wait to go upstairs and start packing. The incident of the couple on the beach was abruptly pushed into the far recesses of her mind.

Bernal found the long drive from Madrid to Málaga tiring; he preferred to go by air everywhere he could, despite the annoying delays at airports which seemed to get worse annually. It was true that he had Consuelo's company, while her brother drove with panache; his car was luxurious and air-conditioned, and Consuelo was a good navigator.

They had left the capital in the early morning and had got to the *albergue* at Antequera in time for lunch. Now reclining in the back of the Mercedes, Bernal was almost overcome by the heavy temptation to take an afternoon doze, but the numerous bends on the mountainous stretch of the N334 through the pass of Las Pedrizas ensured that he was kept awake by jolting from side to side until he felt quite sick. When they began the tortuous descent into Málaga, with glimpses of the shimmering and deeply blue Mediterranean through the ash groves, Bernal leant forward and said: 'It would be best if you dropped me at the Gobierno Civil building in the city centre, because I may get the chance of talking to the Civil Governor before the meeting at seven.'

'That will suit me, too, Luis. I can pick up a hire car at one of the central agencies; they'll have a bigger choice than the branches in the resorts. Shall we come back to fetch you tonight?'

'No need, Consuelo. You have dinner with your famiy and I'll get an official car to run me to Cabo Pino after the meeting is over. It may be a long one, and I shall be expected to accompany the group to see them settled in at Torremolinos.' Bernal had no presentiment of what he was to face that night.

They were now driving through the streets of Málaga, which were already decked out with paper streamers and coloured bunting for the famous annual fair. The Gobierno Civil was an imposing pile standing under the cliff on which rose the impressive walls of the Moorish Alcazaba and high above it the castle of Gibralfaro.

At 5.30 p.m. the heat in the port was stifling, and Bernal began to perspire as he crossed the Plaza de la Aduana in the smoky sunlight. A *calima* or thick heat-haze hung over the entire bay. The sunshine they had enjoyed, from the comfort of the anti-glare windows of the Mercedes, on the higher reaches of the Guadalmedina between the trees of the Cerro de Mallén, had become almost totally obscured. The lack of any breeze and the dusty murky air began to act on Bernal like a threatening augury of what was to come. He wondered why so many rich foreigners had traditionally settled in this torrid climate for reasons of health: perhaps they only spent the winter months here and hastened to more temperate zones in the hottest part of the summer. He smiled as he recalled the old peasants' adage: 'De Virgen a Virgen, fuerte pega el sol'; the month from the Feast of the Virgin of the Dove on 16 July to Assumption Day on 15 August fell within the *canículas* – the dog-days when Sirius rose and set with the sun.

Bernal found the guards at the entrance to the Gobierno Civil half-asleep inside the portico, which was marginally cooler than the shady side of the square. When he showed his gold-star badge they sprang to attention and indicated the main staircase that led to the Civil Governor's door. One of them went to an internal telephone, Bernal noticed, presumably to advise of his arrival.

In the large and well-proportioned office facing the Paseo del Parque and the main inner harbour of the city, Bernal found the provincial governor closeted with the Chief of Police of the city.

'Superintendent Bernal from Madrid! Very delighted to meet you at last. Here we follow all your cases with the greatest interest.'

The Civil Governor shook him warmly by the hand and introduced him to the police chief.

'You have caught us going over the instructions we've received from the Interior Ministry for the mounting of Operación Guardacostas. I see that you have been allotted the most difficult coastal resort in our province, Torremolinos.'

The Chief of Police looked commiserating. 'The inspector in charge there, Jorge Palencia, is very able and bright, and he will provide office accommodation for your group in the Plaza de Andalucía station.'

'That's most reassuring and kind,' said Bernal, 'but may I make a suggestion? This undercover operation is to be carried out in the utmost secrecy. If the ETA commandos are already in place along the Costa del Sol, they may well be keeping a watch on all the police stations in order to observe any special activity and to try to identify the additional personnel the Government may send in. Now, I should prefer to keep my group entirely incognito, if that is possible, without too much contact with the Policía Nacional or the Guardia Civil. Would it be feasible to rent a set of offices in a separate building – with constant telephonic communication with the uniformed forces of course?'

The Governor looked at the Chief of Police, who now replied. 'I take the Chief Superintendent's point. Our *comisarías* can be easily watched, and with the millions of tourists milling round every resort it would be difficult to spot any illegal lookouts the terrorists may have placed, even on this building.'

The Governor glanced nervously out of the large window at the docks traffic now beginning to build up on the Muelle de Heredia. 'I shall authorise it, Comisario, especially since we are assured that the Ministry is going to pay for the whole operation. Otherwise I'm not sure our budget would run to it. What other special measures do you recommend?'

'A complete ban on parked vehicles near public buildings, Governor. Although we have no clue as yet to what form the terrorist threat will take, it's an old trick of theirs to use car-bombs; not just by fixing small bombs with trembler devices to the underside of parked vehicles, but by turning a stolen car into a radio-controlled bomb packed with shrapnel.' He

49

pointed to the line of stationary cars along the kerb of the Paseo del Parque. 'A few kilos of *goma-2* covered with nails in the boot of one of those vehicles would make mincemeat of us.'

The Governor shuddered and crossed himself. 'Very well. A general parking ban. Anything else?'

'Suspect vehicles to be inspected by the bomb-disposal squads before being towed away. I think we should insist on one of the squads being permanently on call here in Málaga, ready to be despatched along the coast in either direction. Then we shall need mine-detectors and sniffer-dogs trained to detect plastic explosive as well as TNT and nitroglycerine.'

'The problem is, Comisario,' said the Chief of Police, 'there aren't enough dogs available to cover all the coastal areas.'

'None the less, the Costa del Sol must be a very high-risk area, as is Alicante. We should try to insist on it. My guess is that as explosions occur the Ministry will be forced to transfer more of these special services from the Basque country to the south and east coasts.'

'But our orders are to prevent any explosions occurring, Superintendent,' said the Governor.

'I must tell you both that I consider our instructions hope-less,' replied Bernal gloomily. 'We have been given the photographs and names and aliases of ten people, and we have been told to check the records of thousands of hotels, boarding-houses and hostels, keep a constant watch on dom-estic and international flights arriving at Rompedizo airport, observe all the passengers coming through the RENFE main railway station here, and those using the branch line along the coast to Fuengirola. But what if the terrorists have already arrived and are holed up in apartments up and down the coast? How will all this surveillance ever find them?'

'We must watch all the roads,' said the Governor, looking ever more alarmed. 'Especially the N334 from Madrid and the N340 Cadiz to Barcelona.'

The police chief shook his head. 'We simply haven't got the manpower.'

'We'll have the manpower,' said the Governor. 'I've asked the Civil Guard to provide the extra road patrols, the Municipal Police to check the roads in all the towns, and the Comandancia de la Marina to increase their surveillance of the harbours and coasts. They are keeping a constant radar watch.'

'Ah,' said Bernal, 'I'm glad you've mentioned that. We must remember that ETA will have thought of all the measures we have mentioned and they'll try to foil them in advance. An approach from the sea can't be ruled out, especially with rubber or fibreglass dinghies which won't show up on radar. There will have to be constant patrols by the coastguards.'

'All the men have been recalled to duty, Comisario, and the Army and Navy put on yellow alert.'

'I've a ghastly notion it won't be enough, any of it,' said Bernal slowly, with a sudden sick feeling. 'I think ETA *Militar* had everything under way before they issued the ultimatum to the Government.'

It was 9.45 p.m. before Bernal and his entire group left the meeting in the Gobierno Civil building in Málaga for Torremolinos. Navarro had arrived in an official chauffeur-driven car from Madrid, accompanied by Juan Lista and Carlos Miranda, so Bernal joined them in the back of the large SEAT limousine, while Elena Fernández, having driven up from Sotogrande in her Renault Fuego, took Ángel Gallardo. He, typically, had cadged a lift from Benidorm to Alicante and from there had travelled on the *coche de línea* to Málaga, arriving somewhat late for the meeting.

Navarro informed them that he had managed to reserve four rooms in the Hotel Paraíso with the help of pressure put on the manager by the local police inspector, Jorge Palencia.

'They are all double rooms, Chief, so we'll allot one to yourself, one to Elena, and the rest of us can share.'

'Don't worry about it, Paco,' commented Bernal, as they merged with the heavy traffic making south on the N340.

'You or Ángel can use my room most of the time. As you know, I'd planned to take a fortnight's holiday in a villa along the coast, so with luck I'll be able to return there each night.'

'If not, Chief, Ángel could probably put up at a *pensión* nearby.'

'Let him have my room for the time being.' Bernal lit a Káiser, and pulled thoughtfully on it. 'We must impress on the hotel manager that this is an undercover operation and that we want to pass ourselves off as ordinary tourists.'

Navarro glanced sideways at his chief and thought that was going to be rather difficult. At least the others were in open-necked shirts and slacks, and he'd noticed that Ángel looked almost punk in wide-cut trousers and a ballooning blouson, while Elena would pass, though she looked somewhat too chic in her expensive Parisian coûture for this part of the Costa del Sol; she would fit in better at Marbella. The real problem was the Superintendent himself: with his bulging lightweight suit and city tie and, above all, his uncanny resemblance to the late Generalísimo on account of his round face, balding dome and greying moustache shaved back from the lip, Navarro considered it impossible for his chief to be viewed as anything other than a figure of authority. He would have to put Elena on to the task of changing her superintendent's appearance.

After they passed Málaga airport at Rompedizo, they ran into a traffic jam on the outskirts of Torremolinos.

'We'll go straight to the hotel, Paco,' said Bernal, 'and claim the rooms. Then you can all get some dinner while I consult with Inspector Palencia.'

Since the official driver wasn't acquainted with the side-roads, they had to make a complete circuit of the town through the Plaza de la Costa del Sol and round the edge of La Nogalera, which was still crowded with tourists at 10.20 p.m. When they reached the narrow Calle de las Mercedes where the Hotel Paraíso stood, it was only to discover that the hotel's private carpark was on the lower cliff-road, which the police driver volunteered to find after dropping them at the main door. At reception the manager received them in person.

'I've managed to vacate two rooms overlooking the sea and two smaller ones facing the street, Comisario. It's a great honour to welcome you to our hotel. We'll all feel much safer.'

'Don't worry about the type of accommodation. Anything you've got will do. I don't expect we'll be in the bedrooms much.' Bernal noticed the sign near the lift indicating the way to the beach. 'Is there a rear exit?'

'Better than that, Superintendent, we have a lift from this lobby down to the underground carpark and the Bajondillo. It will save you walking down the steep path from the town to the Paseo Marítimo.'

'That's very useful,' commented Bernal, who was no lover of steep cliff-paths. He turned to his group, which had now been enlarged by Elena and Ángel. 'You'd better go and eat at once, while I go and find the local inspector.' He went back to the attentive manager, who was hovering in the background. 'Is it far to the *comisaría*?'

'No, Superintendent, it's only a short step to the Plaza de Andalucía. You can go through the shopping arcade in the next street. I'll show you the way.'

The Plaza de Andalucía was a pedestrian precinct, obviously of fairly recent construction, unfinished at its north-eastern end, and surrounded by tall apartment-blocks with shops and bars at street level. There were two large café-terraces where tourists were still eating ice-cream sundaes or taking their after-dinner coffees and brandies, while children raced up and down under the dark ilex trees.

In the gloomier corner of the square Bernal spotted the *comisaría* with a number of brown-painted police jeeps and vans parked outside. Bernal showed his badge to the desk sergeant and was ushered into Inspector Palencia's office.

'It's quiet so far, Comisario, but things will warm up after eleven-thirty, when fights tend to break out in the bars and discos. Today we've had shopliftings and bag-snatchings mostly.'

Bernal filled Palencia in on the main aims of Operación Guardacostas, since the young inspector had been on duty and unable to attend the meeting in Málaga. Palencia listened carefully and then commented: 'We received the mugshots of the eight *etarras* and their two women over the wire yesterday. I've circulated copies to my men and I've placed three shifts of four plain-clothes men in the town, two to watch the RENFE station, and the other on foot patrol.' He pointed to the large wall-map of the area. 'You can see the difficulty of policing this district, Comisario. The shopping area is one large pedestrian precinct, though we can take vehicles in during emergencies. In the mornings this section has a lot of shoppers as well as holidaymakers going through it down to the beaches. Most of the hotels and apartments are on this high ground, so that from eleven a.m. to six p.m. most of the activity is down at the Paseo Marítimo and the foreshore. Then from seven p.m. the cafés, bars, clubs and discothèques on the higher level get the crowds, often until four a.m. or even later. The only really quiet time is from six-thirty to eight-thirty in the morning.'

'When they're all laid out from exhaustion, I suppose,' commented Bernal.

The Inspector smiled. 'I suppose so. Now, there are only two roads suitable for motor-vehicles and both of them run down from the upper level to the Lido at the north-eastern end of the town. A short way beyond the Lido there's Playa Park, a group of new high-rise apartment-blocks built by some of the lesser oil-sheikhs. The promenade is blocked at the south-western end by La Roca, on which the Castillo del Inglés stands. Near that cul-de-sac there is a steep flight of steps leading up to the Garden Suburb past the Hotel Meliá Costa del Sol. On the cliff alongside the hotel is a public lift, but it has been out of action for some years. The Meliá hotel has its own internal lifts for its guests of course. Then in the centre there is the Cuesta del Tago, the most frequented of the cliff-paths, which leads from the end of the Calle de San

54

Miguel in a zigzag down to the beach, coming out near the Bajondillo Apartments.'

'What about La Carihuela, Inspector, is that on your patch?' Bernal pointed to the next resort south-west of Torremolinos.

'I'm afraid it is. The Benalmádena district begins just beyond it. I expect you know it's an old fishing-village famous for its shellfish restaurants and flamenco shows performed on the *azoteas* or flat rooftops, but there's been a lot of commercial development along the front there, so we have to devote quite a lot of manpower to it.' The Inspector asked Bernal about the office accommodation his group would require. 'We can offer you two rooms on the first floor here.'

'That's very kind, but I think it best if I keep my team incognito, away from this *comisaría*. I've been thinking about the Hotel Paraíso. It's well placed, with easy access by lift to the Bajondillo, and it has access roads both to its main entrance and to the underground carpark on the lower level. If the manager has suitable office space for us, we could install ourselves there and get landlines laid to communicate with you here.'

'I think you'll find the manager co-operative. He's an old schoolfriend of mine, so I'll have a word with him.'

At that moment the desk sergeant came rushing in.

'Inspector, there's been a phone call from one of the bar-owners on the Paseo Marítimo. A dead body has been found on the foreshore near La Roca.'

'I'll go down there at once. Have you called the police surgeon?'

'No, but I'll ring him now, and the judge of instruction.'

The Inspector looked at Bernal uncertainly. 'I expect you'll want to get back to your hotel for some dinner, Comisario.'

Bernal felt the sudden excitement of a possible homicide case, and all the tiredness brought on by the long journey and the meeting left him. 'I'll come down with you, if you don't mind, but I don't want to tread on your toes in any way—'

'I'd be greatly honoured. I know you are the leading expert in cases of sudden death.'

A uniformed policeman drove them in one of the brown jeeps via a short cut over an unmade track that ran across a building site from the Avenida del Conde de Mieres down to the Calle de la Bajada, and from there along the Avenida del Lido to the main esplanade. Bernal noticed that most of the commercial premises facing the beach were now shut, including the Montaña Acuática or water-toboggan which had served its last juvenile clients for that day.

At the very end of the Paseo Marítimo the jeep screeched to a halt below the Hotel Meliá, where a small crowd had gathered on the edge of the beach. Inspector Palencia handed Bernal a large torch from the glove-compartment and took another for himself.

'Keep those people back,' he instructed the uniformed man. 'Try to get them to disperse if you can, once we've located the witnesses.'

There was no street-lighting at the place where the body lay. The two police officers went up to the group of a dozen holidaymakers and shone torches in their faces.

'Which of you found the body?'

'I did,' said a middle-aged man wearing Bermuda shorts. 'I got the bar-owner from over there, and he called you when we could see there was no hope of bringing the man round. He's only a young chap, too.'

The bar-owner now joined them. 'I've called an ambulance, but there's no sign of life.'

'Did any of you see him fall?' asked Bernal.

No one volunteered any information except for the middle-aged Spaniard.

'I stumbled over him when I went to look for my small boy's tennis-ball which he lost in the dark. The children were playing at the foot of the steps over there. I didn't see anyone near the body.'

Inspector Palencia bent over the corpse, which lay on its left side, turned away from him. It was dressed in a blue patterned shirt and jeans. He felt carefully for a pulse in the right wrist but could find none. 'The clothing's dry,' he reported to Bernal, 'so he hasn't been in the water. The body's still very warm.'

Bernal stood alongside him, shining his torch towards the beach and the rocks. Palencia went to the other side of the corpse to light up the face.

'My God,' he whispered to Bernal in a shaky voice, 'it's one of my own plain–clothes men. He was on duty on these steps leading down from the Garden Suburb.' He knelt down and placed his ear against the man's chest and listened. 'There's no respiration or heartbeat.'

'Any visible injuries?' asked Bernal.

'Nothing to be seen. No sign of a wound.'

'It may be in the scalp,' said Bernal.

'A blow on the head, you think?'

'Could be. He may have died of a skull-fracture.'

Palencia began to explore the hair of the dead man with his fingers.

'Better leave it for the surgeon,' said Bernal gently.

'We tried artificial respiration for more than fifteen minutes,' volunteered the bar-owner, 'as well as mouth-to-mouth resuscitation, but there was no response.'

'So you had to move the body. How was it lying when you first saw it?' asked Bernal.

The middle-aged holidaymaker now spoke. 'Almost face-down, with the head slightly turned to the right, but in that same place.'

Bernal swept the beam of his torch on to the sand around the corpse, but it was all hopelessly scuffed. 'Did you see anyone coming away from this part of the beach when you went to look for the tennis-ball?'

'No, no one, and I didn't find the ball, either.'

Palencia took out a notebook and asked the witnesses for their names and addresses, telling them they would be required to make depositions for the judge of instruction.

'Get on to the radio and see what's happened to that surgeon,' the Inspector told the uniformed man.

Bernal looked at the cars parked on each side of the Paseo Marítimo some thirty metres away and turned to the bar-owner. 'Did you see anyone driving off in a vehicle from in front of your bar?'

'I was in and out, serving the customers sitting outside. Cars came and went, but I didn't pay any particular attention. A lot come as far as this to turn.' He pointed towards the beach. 'I didn't see anyone coming up from there. It's too late now for any bathers.'

'But did you notice anyone going away from this point, towards the rocks?'

'You can't get past there, sir; the sea covers the lower rocks most of the time, and there's a sheer drop from the Castillo del Inglés above.' He pointed towards the dark bulk of the cliff above them. 'No one could get to La Carihuela by the shore, unless they went in a boat.'

Bernal went back to Palencia, who was still kneeling by the body of his dead officer. 'It might be worth sending for more men to search the beach. And you'll need the police photographer. Your man hasn't been dead long, and you must treat it as a suspicious death. It's unlikely that a healthy young policeman dropped dead of a heart-attack.'

The Inspector went back to the jeep to call for reinforcements, just as the headlights of a car turning at the end of the promenade raked the apparently deserted beach. The police surgeon hurried across to them and greeted the Inspector, who introduced Superintendent Bernal. The doctor opened his bag and took out a stethoscope; loosening the shirt, he auscultated the chest of the dead man.

'Get these people away if you can. I want to take the rectal temperature. He hasn't been dead for very long, I think.' He handed the Inspector an air thermometer. 'Please check that for me. I'll try to calculate the time that has elapsed since the moment of decease.'

While the uniformed man moved the spectators back to the promenade, Bernal began to walk along the beach towards the rocky point, moving his flashlight carefully from side to side as he went. There were myriad footprints in the sand from the hundreds of holidaymakers who had crossed and recrossed it during the day and, he judged, during many days past, since the high tide didn't reach this part of the beach – at least not in summer, it seemed.

Suddenly Bernal stumbled on a pile of sand and nearly fell into a large hole dug near the lower rocks. Children had probably been making sand-castles, he supposed. As he was about to pass on, towards the water's edge, he shone the torch back into the hole and examined the sides of it. The dug-out sand was still very wet, which surprised him, since it had been dark for over two hours and it seemed unlikely that children would have been there so late. He noticed that the sides of the hole bore the marks of a large spade. Would children have used an implement as wide as that? He knelt at the side of the hole where he could see something gleaming. Taking out a penknife, he worked the shiny object loose. It was an empty cockleshell, nothing more. Using the knife carefully, Bernal prodded the base of the hole, which measured more than half a metre across and nearly half a metre deep, but he found nothing further. He observed how squarely the hole was cut, almost as though it had contained a box of some kind. Hardly children's work, he considered. He moved on, looking for further signs of excavation, but saw none.

He could now see an ambulance and a large black car approaching at speed along the Paseo Marítimo, and he began to make his way back to the spot where the body lay. As he passed the pile of sand and the hole, he ran his torch over the place again, and spotted a small white object he had missed the first time. He touched it with his penknife and recognised it to be a cigarette-butt. He felt in his jacket pocket for a pair of tweezers and a small plastic bag. Carefully retrieving the butt, he sniffed at the tobacco. Black, possibly a Ducado to judge by the white filter-tip. He placed it in the bag in case it should be needed for forensic examination; it would bear saliva traces.

He could see that the judge of instruction had now arrived on the scene, as well as the police photographer, who made eerie magnesium flashes that lit the whole area in stark whiteness. In its distant reflection Bernal thought he could see among the distant sunshades a pair of dark figures making off along the shore towards the Lido. He went back to the official group where Inspector Palencia presented him to the judge, who now authorised the lifting of the body for autopsy in the public mortuary at Málaga.

'We should try to keep this out of the press,' Bernal murmured to Palencia. 'Perhaps the post-mortem could be carried out at the military hospital?'

The judge readily agreed to this proposal, and now they all watched as the ambulancemen placed the corpse on a stretcher. Pressed in the sand under it was a small black walkie-talkie radio.

'Do your plain-clothes patrols call in at fixed times, Palencia?'

The Inspector looked at the sand-covered radio and bent to pick it up.

'No, better leave it,' warned Bernal. 'Ask the photographer to come over. I also want him to take shots of a hole dug in the sand near the rocks.'

When the pocket transceiver had been photographed *in situ* from various angles, Bernal produced a piece of string and eased it in a loop round the radio, tying it firmly.

'Now take it back suspended like this for fingerprinting,' he urged. 'Don't wrap it in anything or any latent prints will get smudged. It would be better to hang it in a small cardboard box to get to the forensic lab safely. Are these transmitters standard issue?'

'No, Comisario, they were brought in especially for under-cover work, because they'll fit into the pocket of a pair of jeans without causing too much of a bulge. The men call in as near as possible to each hour, or at once in an emergency. They can't communicate with one another, only with Central Control. They are told to choose a secluded place when they call in, naturally. And we don't call them, for obvi-ous reasons.'

'But he didn't call in, even though he had some kind of emergency.'

'No, he can't have done, or the *cabo* in charge of the radio-room would have informed me.'

'Are the men armed?'

'They have the option of carrying a small revolver, but I think most of them decided not to, because of the difficulty of concealing it under summer clothing.'

'You'd better order the others to go armed from now on,' said Bernal grimly.

Palencia was clearly very deeply upset. 'Antonio García was one of my best men.'

'Get your uniformed men to search all this part of the beach as far as those sunshades.' Bernal pointed north-eastwards.

'What should they be looking for?'

'Tell them to collect everything, including all refuse, and put it in plastic bags. It would be best if they used ropes to mark out the area in squares, and number them and the corresponding bags. Have you any metal-detectors?'

'No, but I'll ask Málaga to send what they've got.'

'You may have to leave that until first light, but it's urgent to complete the search as quickly as possible, before the early-morning bathers arrive. It's bound to attract public attention if you have to cordon off the beach for long. I suggest you place a guard along this whole stretch for the night.'

Palencia gave these instructions to the uniformed men who had now arrived in a police van.

'I'll tell my driver to take you up to your hotel, Comisario. You must be exhausted after such a long day.'

'Strangely I don't feel a bit tired. It will hit me later on, I expect.'

Bernal took Palencia by the arm and shook his hand. 'I'm extremely sorry about the loss of your agent. I promise you we'll get to the bottom of it, however long it takes.'

Palencia, who couldn't be more than thirty-five, Bernal thought, suddenly looked very young and vulnerable. 'Thank you. I must go and break the news to Antonio's wife.' His voice choked, and then he recovered. 'They say you've never failed in a case yet, Superintendent.'

61

'That's what they say, but one day I'll publish a book about all my failures.'

Back at the Hotel Paraíso, Bernal found Paco Navarro waiting anxiously for him in the lobby.

'I rang the *comisaría* and they said you'd gone to view a suspected homicide down on the beach. Is it a case for us, *jefe*?'

'I'm not sure yet, but we're involved, whether it concerns the Basque terrorists or not. The dead man is one of Palencia's plain-clothes men.'

It was very late when the powerfully built stranger emerged to feed the wild-cats which prowled on the rooftops of the Bajondillo. They thronged round his legs and jumped with expectation as he unwrapped the plastic-covered parcel.

'Now, don't scratch me,' he admonished as they clawed at his trousers. 'There's plenty for all of you.'

Leaving them to fight and screech over the pile of evil-smelling offal, he turned and began to climb the steep path that led up to the Calle de San Miguel. What foreign waif would he find needing his assistance tonight? he asked himself. He stopped to light up a Winston by the railings near the Windmill restaurant and looked casually down at the beach. His eyes narrowed when he saw the bright arc-lamps shining along the sand towards La Roca and the flashing blue lights on the roofs of the stationary police cars. Suddenly he tensed as he saw a fair-haired youth come staggering slowly down the steps. Perhaps he had a customer straight away tonight.

It was later still when the police driver dropped Bernal off at El Puerto de Cabo Pino, where they had some difficulty at first in locating Consuelo's brother-in-law's duplex apartment. He found Consuelo waiting up, and she prepared a sandwich for him in the kitchen, where he recounted to her the surprising turn of events at Torremolinos.

'Will you call me early – say, at seven-thirty – Chelo? The driver will be returning for me at eight.'

'It's worse than being at work in Madrid, Luchi. I thought we'd come down here for a complete rest.'

'That may be delayed now, love, with the death of a policeman to investigate.'

The bright sunshine that heralded Tuesday, 3 August, the day when ETA *Militar*'s ultimatum to the Government was to expire at noon, woke Bernal up before Consuelo, and he felt extremely relaxed by the warm sea-breeze blowing gently in through the half-open shutters. Without making a sound, he slipped on a dressing-gown and went out on to the balcony to take his first look at Cabo Pino in the daylight.

The architect had planned the yachting marina and exclusive holiday-village more tastefully than was usual in such developments, he thought. He noted the presence of three large sea-going yachts tied up at the mole, and glimpsed a few early bathers at the water's edge on the long beach that extended to a distant point on the south-eastern horizon.

Bernal turned back to take a rapid shave in the elegantly fitted *en suite* bathroom and, after donning a new beige light-weight suit and matching tie he had recently treated himself to in Celso García's, he crept downstairs to make himself a coffee before the official car came for him. He wanted to be in Málaga in time to attend the autopsy on the dead policeman.

As soon as the car arrived, Bernal let himself quietly out of the elegant duplex apartment. The large SEAT zoomed up the steep hill past the road-barrier that shut off this private village from all public traffic, and soon emerged on to the N340. Fortunately there was very little traffic at that hour, and they sped through Fuengirola without difficulty.

When half an hour later they were passing through Benalmádena, Bernal instructed the driver to turn into Torremolinos and go to the *comisaría*. If Inspector Palencia hadn't left, he would offer him a lift.

As they drove into the Plaza de Andalucía, Bernal spotted the local inspector coming out of the building, looking worried and clutching an official file.

'Shall we drive over to Málaga together, Inspector?' Bernal called out.

'Thank you, Superintendent. That will save me taking one of the jeeps. I can't spare any men this morning.'

In the back seat of the SEAT 134, Bernal offered him a Káiser, which Palencia declined in favour of one of his own Winstons. He showed Bernal a telex message he had just received from the Gobierno Civil in Málaga.

'We had an earlier enquiry sent on from Interpol last week about three youths who had been on holiday in Torremolinos reported missing by their families. I've got the earlier telex for you to see in this file.' He searched out the relevant piece of paper. 'Now it appears that there are two more missing youths, one Italian and one German. Their next of kin haven't heard from them for over a week, though they were expected to return home before now. Five of the foreign consuls at Málaga have been in touch with the Civil Governor to ask him to have enquiries made about the whereabouts of their missing nationals, and he's asked the Chief of Police to take urgent action. You'll realise, with the investigation into the death of my agent and the whole business of mounting Operación Guardacostas, that I simply haven't got the necessary men.'

'You can only cover those operations for which you have the manpower, Palencia, but you can count on the help of my group and myself. Can I see the first message from Interpol?'

Bernal read the original request for information about the French youth called Jean-Paul Morillon, the Dutch boy Henke Visserman, and the Londoner Henry Marks. Afterwards he remained silent, but looked grave. Then he picked up that day's message from the Málaga police headquarters referring to the various consuls' enquiries about the first three cases, plus the new request from the Italian consul to trace Salvatore Croce, aged twenty, a factory-worker from Milan, last heard of in Torremolinos on 24 July. He had been travelling alone for a fortnight's holiday on the Costa del Sol and he'd sent home a postcard franked on that date

64

which had taken a week to reach his parents' address. He had been due home on 29 July on an Alitalia charter flight from Málaga airport, but his father, who had been waiting for him at Milan, had been informed by the airline that Salvatore had failed to check in.

'The Italian consul hasn't informed the Gobierno Civil where this youth was staying in Torremolinos, Palencia. If he had a return ticket on a charter flight, wouldn't that have included a hotel room in the fare?'

'Not necessarily, Superintendent. Many of these young holidaymakers buy the tickets at the last moment at a cut-price rate, and that leaves them free to hitch-hike down the coast, putting up at cheap hostels or even sleeping rough on the beaches. We get a huge floating population all through the summer months – this is the *turismo barato* that Fraga when he was Minister of Tourism tried to prevent – and these kids are pretty restless, commonly spending only two or three nights in each resort.'

'Now, this fifth case of the German youth is more promising,' commented Bernal. 'Friedrich Albert Keller rang up his elder brother in Frankfurt only four days ago and told him he had booked a room in the Lido Apartments for his last two nights before catching the return Lufthansa charter flight on Sunday evening, since his money was running out. Earlier he had been in Marbella and Fuengirola. There is a similar pattern: his elder brother went to the airport to meet him off the flight, only to discover that his brother hadn't checked in at Málaga. Unlike the other four cases, here we've got the name of the place he stayed in.'

'I spotted that, Comisario, and I've sent my *cabo* down there to interview the manager. This passport photo they've sent by wire isn't very clear, but we've got his name and passport number. The staff at the Lido Apartments should have made out a police registration-card the day he booked in there.'

'It is a very intriguing affair, Palencia,' Bernal mused. 'No doubt you get tourists going missing each month, especially young hippie types who drift about the world.'

'We do get enquiries occasionally, but they usually turn up sooner or later and return to the bosom of their family if the money runs out, or when autumn comes and they decide to go back to work if they can find any. But some of them go on via Almería to Ceuta and cross the frontier into Morocco, especially if they're drug-takers or want to try their luck at drug-smuggling; often they don't return to the Peninsula. When young girls are involved we do all the tracing we can, in case they've been lured into prostitution or even been shipped off to North Africa into the residual white-slave trade.'

'But girls don't often go on holiday alone, do they?' questioned Bernal. 'In my experience they always travel in pairs or larger groups for safety.' He riffled through the file again. 'Now, what strikes me about these five missing youths is that they were all travelling alone, since there's no mention in any of the reports of a travelling companion. That's surprising, but not altogether implausible. Boys of that age who may be loners or too shy to have permanent friends may expect to make friends along the way in the resorts they visit. That's what the postwar international mobility of young people has brought: this new freedom to roam the world at little expense. We're the ones who get the headaches when things go wrong.' He lit up another Káiser and pulled on it. 'In these cases there is a connecting thread: they all contacted their families at some point, either by sending a postcard or by telephoning them from Torremolinos, and then they all failed to check in for their flight at Málaga airport, thereby losing a considerable amount of money on their return charter ticket presumably. After that their families have heard no more from them. It's very ominous, Palencia.'

'You mean there might be a new kind of masculine white-slave traffic, perhaps to North Africa? We've had one or two problems with the minor oil-sheikhs down in the new high-rise towers in that respect, mainly with local youths.'

'You'd better let me see the details of those cases when we get back. We may have to pay a call on some of your Arab residents.' Bernal drew on his cigarette. 'Or it may be

66

something worse.' The old detective suddenly felt in his bones that all the disappearances could be interrelated and that there might be a maniac at large. 'But don't let's look on the black side yet, Palencia. Your corporal may bring back some news of the German youth, at least.'

The driver of the official car negotiated with skill the morning traffic in the centre of Málaga, and soon Bernal and Palencia were being driven along the Calle de la Victoria and from there up the Calle de Amargura to the old military hospital, a large building that stood in front of the church that housed the patron saint of the city, Our Lady of the Victory.

There they made their way to the mortuary where the local police pathologist had begun the post-mortem examination of Antonio García. The smell of formalin and putrefaction that hung heavily over the white-tiled room caused Bernal's stomach to churn as usual, and he turned so pale that Palencia suggested they go to take a coffee until the pathologist called them with some news.

When they were ensconced in the visitors' canteen, the young inspector persuaded Bernal to have a Carlos III brandy with his coffee.

'It's the first time I've ever lost an agent on duty, Comisario.'

'These things happen, Palencia, especially in times of terrorism.'

'You think he was killed by the *etarras*, then?'

'We'll have to wait and see what the pathologist comes up with, but it's very hard to believe that a young and healthy policeman would drop down dead on duty.'

Over an hour passed before they were sent for. In the mortuary office they were confronted by a very puzzled pathologist.

'There's no sign of any disease in the organs. I've taken cross-sections of the cardiac arteries and examined them under the high-powered microscope. There's no trace of an infarct or embolism.' The police surgeon took out a Havana cigar and began to trim the end of it. 'Likewise there are no signs of petechiæ in the lungs or anywhere else that would indicate asphyxia. Your man seems to have been entirely healthy. I'll send the organs for laboratory analysis of course. That will show if there's any kind of drug or poison. My guess is that he died of a vagal inhibition which caused sudden and irreversible cardiac arrest. But I cannot find any external injury that could have produced it.'

'What about the scalp, Doctor?' asked Bernal. 'Is there no injury there?'

'I've gone over it centimetre by centimetre and can find nothing. I'll have to proceed to examine the brain for signs of haemorrhaging. My assistant is preparing it for inspection now.'

'How soon will you be able to tell us?' asked Palencia, who was clearly very distressed.

'In half an hour or so I'll be able to give you a preliminary opinion.'

'We'll wait, Doctor.'

After forty minutes had passed, the surgeon re-emerged with a large textbook in his hands, looking somewhat less nonplussed.

'I've found minor haemorrhaging at the back of the brain stem, but there's absolutely no external injury to account for it, so it doesn't seem to be traumatic in origin. I've just been checking in the textbooks, and we may be faced with one of those extremely rare cases of cerebral haemorrhage which they tell us can occur at any age and which show little or no trace at autopsy. I'll order a full microscopic examination of the brain cells of course.'

Bernal gave signs of not being very convinced by this explanation and looked at Palencia. 'Would there be any objection to bringing down Doctor Peláez from Madrid to give a further opinion?'

'I'd be very relieved if that could be arranged, Comisario,' said the local pathologist. 'I've never seen a case like this one, and Doctor Peláez is the greatest pathologist in the country. It would be an honour to have him here. In the meantime

I'll have everything carefully refrigerated and start some tests in the lab.'

Bernal and Palencia left the military hospital more worried than when they had arrived, and Bernal determined to have Navarro locate Peláez at the earliest opportunity and ask him to take the next available flight to Málaga.

News of the first bomb-explosions on the tourist beaches began to reach the Anti-Terrorist Unit in Madrid shortly after 3 p.m. on that day, Tuesday, 3 August. The ultimatum issued by ETA *Militar* had expired at noon without any reply having been sent by the Spanish Government.

Bernal sat in Inspector Palencia's office in the Plaza de Andalucía in Torremolinos reading the telex messages transmitted from the capital via the Gobierno Civil in Málaga. The first report had come in from the Catalan police at 3.05 p.m.: a small bomb had exploded in the sand near the promenade at Lloret de Mar. Fortunately most of the holidaymakers had left the beach to take lunch in their hotels, and the only people nearby were the deck-chair attendants and ice-cream vendors. No one had been injured, but there was some damage to the base of the steps leading down from the esplanade. The beach had been cordoned off and army bomb-disposal experts summoned to examine the evidence and determine the type of explosive and fuse mechanism used.

This report had been rapidly followed by another from the Alicante police. At 3.12 p.m. a bomb had gone off on the beach near the fishing port, just below the Apartotel Meliá, and it had left a large crater in the sand. Some palm trees on the Paseo Marítimo were damaged, as were some beach umbrellas and deck-chairs, but because of the time of day no holidaymaker had been injured.

The third report had reached Madrid at 3.20 p.m., from Marbella. An explosion had occurred near a *chiringuito* or beach-hut restaurant, which had been caught by the blast. A number of people lunching inside had received injuries from the falling wooden beams that had supported the light roof made of dried palm-fronds which collapsed on to the tables. None of the clients was seriously injured, but a waitress had been taken to Marbella hospital with head wounds.

These messages, Bernal saw, were accompanied by a stream of orders from the Chief Comisario in Madrid to each of the provincial police forces to find out as quickly as possible from the army experts how the devices had been triggered. In case they were radio-controlled, Madrid had ordered cordons to be thrown round the three resorts so far affected in order to trap the terrorists as they tried to make their getaway. All vehicles were to be thoroughly searched for illicit radio transmitters.

Bernal handed the messages back to Inspector Palencia. 'It's not going to be easy to foil them, Palencia. I feared from the beginning that they had made their preparations before issuing the ultimatum to the Government. Their commandos are probably installed at a number of points along the coast. If they have hired apartments and have planted the bombs nearby, no road-block will ever trap them, since they can sit pretty on their balconies and set off the bombs whenever they like. The only slight consolation so far is that there have been no fatalities. It seems they want to alarm the foreign tourists, but not kill them.'

'Assuming they're using the same method here as in those other resorts, Comisario, shouldn't I call Málaga and ask for experts with more metal-detectors to scan the main beaches?' He fell silent for a moment. 'What about the danger to my men who are at this very moment searching the scene where the body of my plain-clothes man was found last night?'

'Yes, you're right, of course. Call them off at once until we can get some army experts here. You get them on the car radio while I contact Madrid and ask for immediate assistance. We'd also better ask the Guardia Civil to arrange for the road-blocks that Madrid will surely ask for if we get an explosion here.' Bernal looked suddenly grave. 'I'm also worried about the danger to the bomb-detection men when the terrorists spot them going over the beaches with mine-detectors. Really we should wait until after dark.'

'But that might be too late,' Palencia objected.

'With such an enormous area to cover, it's too late anyway. Assuming the *etarras* have already put their bombs in position here, there are four ways they may be set off: either by contact or a trembler device, or by a pre-set timer, or by remote control. The last method requires a visual fix on the hidden bombs if they are going to be exploded either to injure a uniformed policeman, or alternatively not to injure an innocent tourist or a child.' Bernal took a sudden decision. 'Let's clear the beaches for the rest of the day, Inspector, and place a cordon along the Paseo Marítimo. After all, most people go to the beach in the mornings. They'll have started to wander back to their hotels and apartments about now.'

'What about sending men to scan the windows and balconies overlooking the beach, Comisario? They might spot someone holding a radio transmitter.'

'It would be a very long shot, Palencia, but you could put your plain-clothes men on to it.' Bernal thought for a moment. 'The beach will have to be taped out in squares as soon as it's dark — starting, I suggest, with the strip nearest the esplanade. Of course the experts will have to use torches, but we should avoid the further use of arc-lamps in order to reduce the danger.'

'When we close off the beaches, there'll certainly be an outcry from the mayor and the hoteliers and traders if the tourists are deprived for long.'

'You'll have to tell them to choose between their clients' losing their suntans or their lives. We must ask the army experts whether there's a way of jamming the radio signals the terrorists might use.'

'There probably is, Comisario, but wouldn't it interfere with our own radio communications, as well as with those of the coastguards, ambulancemen and fire brigade, not to mention the commercial radios such as those of the taxi firms?'

'I'm going to phone Madrid, Inspector, and ask for my usual technician, Varga, to bring his team down here at once.

We're going to need the very best technical assistance. Once we have news of the type of device used in the other resorts, he and the bomb squad may come up with a solution. In the meantime, let's keep our options open by shutting off the beaches right now.'

Palencia's *cabo*, a stout officer whose formidable physique threatened to burst from his beige shirt and brown trousers, halted his jeep on the corner of Martín Pescador. He strode through the terrace of the restaurant crowded with tourists taking lunch and entered the whitewashed gates of the Lido Apartments. It was just like a motel without the cars, he thought: two-storeyed rows of chalets joined together on three sides of a grassy plot which was showing the brown signs of drought. He made for the manager's office and gave a loud and peremptory knock. Entering at once, he found only a youth in bathing-trunks reading an adult comic who sprang to his feet guiltily when he saw the police uniform.

'Can I help you?'

'Is the manager here?'

'He's taking an afternoon nap, I think.'

'You'd better fetch him.'

The manager, who entered the office alone, turned out to be a worried-looking man in his late thirties who constantly ran his fingers through his tousled hair.

'What can I do for you, Officer?'

'Please get out your registration-cards for the past week. We need to find the one filled in by a West German youth' – the *cabo* took out a report sheet from his shirt pocket and stumbled over the foreign name – 'Friedrich – Albert – Keller. The surname is spelt with a K .'

The manager opened a grey filing-cabinet, the contents of which spilled out in considerable disorder.

'We get a lot of young foreigners who only book in for a night or two.'

'And very profitable it is for you, too,' commented the policeman. 'I hope you fill in cards for them all.'

'Yes, yes, of course,' he replied nervously. 'We keep them until your people come to collect them.' He placed a loose bundle of the small white cards on the desk. 'What was the date of arrival?'

'The thirtieth of July, or thereabouts, for two nights.'

The manager went through the cards one by one, with the *cabo* looking over his shoulder.

'They aren't in any sequence,' he remarked disapprovingly.

'No, but I've been meaning to tidy them up before the weekend.' The manager reached the last card. 'I'm afraid there isn't one here in the name of Keller.'

'But there's nowhere else called the Lido Apartments, is there?'

'Well, no, but there are a number of lodging-houses over the shops on the Avenida del Lido.'

The *cabo* now produced the rather muzzy photograph of the blond German youth that was sent over the wire by Interpol. 'Do you recognise him?' He observed the manager's facial reactions carefully.

'It's difficult to tell. We get so many foreigners here who frequent the Poseidón beach establishment opposite. None of them stays longer than a fortnight, usually far less.'

'You'd better look through your records again. Did you have anyone who checked in on the thirtieth of July and checked out by Sunday the first of August?'

The manager took out of the desk drawer a large battered book that contained a chart of the twenty-four rooms with overlapping pages opposite for each week of the year. The squares were filled in with pencilled scribblings of foreign names, with many crossings-out.

'I don't understand how you can keep track of when a room's booked and when it's free, using this system,' remarked the policeman disapprovingly.

'Oh, I can follow it, but the night porter sometimes messes it up when he lets a room after I go off duty at eight p.m. I always make sure the clients sign the registration-cards and I

73

keep their passports until the next day so that I can fill in all the details.'

'That also stops them going off without paying, I suppose.'

'We usually ask for the money or traveller's cheque in advance.'

'But the night porter, does he always get them to sign the cards and keep their passport?'

'He's supposed to.'

The *cabo* was suspicious, realising that the rooms could be let for a night, without the management being aware of the fact, for a quick buck to be made, though he supposed that the person in charge at night would have to square it with the chambermaid.

'Were any rooms vacant on the night of the thirtieth?'

The manager pored over the disastrously kept planner. 'There was one. Room fourteen across the way. It's the least popular room because it adjoins the bar-terrace next door.'

'So the night porter could have rented it out without your knowing?'

'I'm sure he wouldn't do such a thing! He's been with us for many years, and his wife also works here as a chambermaid.'

That would make it much easier to pull off, thought the policeman.

'He certainly couldn't have let it for more than a night without my finding out,' the manager added confidently.

'What's his name and address? We'll have to question all the other staff as well and show them this photograph.'

The manager took out a wages-book from the desk drawer and copied out the names and addresses for the *cabo*. 'The only other staff, apart from the night porter and his wife, are two other women who clean the rooms and take the laundry home to wash each day.'

'What about the young man who was here when I arrived?'

'Oh, he just looks after the garden and does odd jobs in exchange for a room.'

'Let's see if he can recognise the German youth in this photo.'

'What's he done? What do you want him for?'

'I can't say. It's an enquiry from Interpol.'

Bernal had arranged a full conference with his team for 5 p.m. in the Hotel Paraíso. He still wanted to keep them, as far as possible, incognito, so he asked Inspector Palencia to join them discreetly, as though he was merely dropping in on his old schoolfriend, the hotel manager. This personage had done them proud, thought Bernal, as he entered the first-floor conference room, the long windows of which afforded a spectacular view of the sea. He saw that Navarro had organised a makeshift office for them, with telephones already installed at each table. A large map of Málaga province had been placed on the long wall facing the windows, as well as a smaller political map of the entire Iberian Peninsula and a large-scale street-plan of the Torremolinos police district.

When all the members of his group were assembled, Bernal began by giving them a summary of the latest news from Madrid about the explosions in the other resorts.

'So far there have been no explosions here in Málaga province, but a pattern is emerging elsewhere. The bombs were made of one or two kilos of *goma-2* plastic explosive, and they were all buried in shallow sand near the promenades. It has been concluded from the fuse mechanism recovered almost intact at Lloret that they are being set off by remote control.'

'It's surprising that none has gone off along this part of the coast, Chief,' commented Navarro. 'One would have thought it would be a prime target.'

'I think we must work on the assumption that some have been put into position on these beaches, too, Paco. Inspector Palencia, who will be joining us shortly, has asked for metal-detectors to be sent from Málaga in order to begin a scan of the beaches as soon as it's dark. In the mean time, I've suggested that the foreshore be cordoned off.'

Bernal half-turned and looked out of the long window, through which they all had a panoramic view of a line of uniformed men clearing holidaymakers from the beach in front of the Bajondillo Apartments. They could see the attendants gathering up the *tumbonas* and deck-chairs and pulling back the coloured awnings.

'Does the Anti-Terrorist Squad in Madrid know how long ago the bombs were planted?' asked Ángel.

'They say there's no way of knowing.'

'It's just that I recall seeing a man and a woman digging in the sand at Benidorm after dusk the day before yesterday, *jefe*. At the time I assumed they were digging for shellfish. Have any explosions taken place there?'

Bernal looked through the telex messages he had received from Madrid. 'Apparently not, Ángel. You'd better get on the phone at once and talk to the superintendent in charge there, giving him the exact location. A metal-detector could then be used to find the device, if that's what it was.'

'I saw something, too, at Sotogrande, Chief,' said Elena, 'as I was returning to my father's house the night before last. Again it was a man and a woman coming up to the promenade from the beach and driving off in a car. The man was carrying a spade. I thought it strange at the time, since there are no shellfish to be found there.'

'You also had better phone the officer in charge – it'll be the superintendent at La Línea. Sotogrande is in Cadiz province, isn't it?' Elena nodded. 'Tell the superintendents both at Benidorm and at La Línea that I suggest they wait until dark before trying to locate the supposed bombs, in case the terrorists blow up members of the bomb-disposal squads when they approach the sites.'

While Ángel and Elena were phoning, Inspector Palencia arrived looking very keyed up.

'There have been three more explosions this afternoon, Comisario. We've just received a telex message via Málaga. All were of the same type of device as the ones that exploded earlier in the day.'

'Any of them in our area?' asked Bernal anxiously.

'No, sir. One was at Cadaqués in Catalonia, the second was at Gandía in Valencia province, and the third on the Playa de San Juan at Alicante.'

'So they're hitting all types of resort,' mused Bernal, 'elegant ones as well as popular ones.'

'I've asked the communications room at Málaga to pass on all messages to you here, sir, now your lines are linked up, as well as to my station.'

'I'll check that we've got the link to Málaga, Chief,' said Navarro.

'What about a protected line to Madrid, Paco?'

'Telefónica has connected up a line separate from the hotel's lines, Chief, and I'm waiting for the technician to come and fit the scrambler phone.'

Ángel and Elena now returned from making their calls, and Bernal asked them if there was any news from Benidorm or La Línea.

'The superintendent at La Línea has sent out an army squad to Sotogrande, Chief,' replied Elena. 'I've given him an exact description of the spot. I passed on your advice about waiting for cover of darkness, but he says he's prepared to search all the dwellings there for the terrorists before he lets the bomb-disposal men on to the beach.'

'Is that feasible?' asked Bernal. 'Could he search every building facing the sea or with a view of the promenade?'

'It would take a lot of men, but it could be done, Chief.'

'Let's hope it won't come to that here. It would take a couple of hundred men a number of days, and it might be ineffective if the terrorists are vehicle-based and are just travelling from resort to resort letting off the bombs they planted earlier.'

'Shouldn't we use the road-blocks, then, Superintendent?' asked Palencia. 'The Civil Guard patrols have been issued with the mugshots of the terrorists and they could also search all vehicles for radio transmitters.'

'It's worth considering, Palencia,' said Bernal thoughtfully. 'There presumably aren't enough operatives in the terrorist hit-squads for them to be in every resort at once, so maybe they have had to move from place to place, not only to plant the devices but also to explode them later. Perhaps they have regional safe houses, at five or six points along the east and south-east coasts.' He looked at the map of the Peninsula, where Paco Navarro had placed red discs marked with the time and date to indicate where the explosions had occurred so far.

'It's noticeable that they haven't hit this part of the Costa del Sol yet,' said Lista. 'If they've got safe houses, they could be situated in the large cities such as Barcelona, Valencia and Alicante.'

'I think we've got good reason to think they're in Málaga as well,' said Bernal. And then with sudden decision he turned to Palencia and said: 'Let's activate the Guardia Civil road-controls and searches now. They might produce something. You'd better explain to them about looking for small radio transmitters.'

After Palencia had returned from the telephone, Bernal invited him to give the whole team a detailed account of how the body of his plain-clothes man, Antonió García, had been discovered the night before near the end of the Paseo Marítimo, and the inconclusive result of the autopsy. They all listened gravely as the local inspector, with obvious emotion, gave them his account. 'I must admit to being completely baffled by it,' he ended, 'and I ask myself whether his death is related to that of the five missing foreign holidaymakers, or to the terrorist activity, or to neither.'

'Until Doctor Peláez arrives this evening and performs a second autopsy, I don't think we'll get much further', said Bernal, 'because of the admittedly faint possibility that he died of natural causes.'

'Isn't it probable that his death, if it was violent, was related to the terrorists?' asked Navarro. 'After all, his body was discovered on the edge of a lonely section of the foreshore after dark.'

'That's precisely what I had tentatively concluded, Paco,' answered Bernal. 'Last night I noticed a hole dug in the sand not far from where Palencia's man was found. A possible reconstruction is that he saw someone digging in the sand after dark and went to investigate. On being surprised, the terrorists then eliminated him. The question is: how did they do it without leaving a mark on the body?'

'These disappearing foreign youths, Chief,' asked Ángel, 'you don't think they could be connected with the ETA bombing campaign?'

'I hadn't thought so, Ángel, but now you raise it I see that it's not entirely impossible. I suppose the *etarras* could have decided to take some foreigners hostage in order to reinforce their demands and, of course, to seek more international publicity and deter foreign tourists from coming to Spain.'

Elena was looking puzzled. 'But in that case wouldn't the victims have been of different backgrounds, Chief? In all the kidnappings that have taken place in the Basque country, those abducted have either been rich industrialists who refused to pay what ETA calls the "political tax", or VIPs such as Julio Iglesias' father whom they held for ransom. Yet none of these missing youths comes from a rich or important family as far as we know, do they?'

'You're quite right, of course, Elena, but we mustn't rule anything out. It could just be a new ploy to gain publicity throughout Europe: you've noticed that the five youths are all from different countries? When the foreign newspapers get wind of a series of disappearances they'll blow it up into a front-page story. Perhaps the terrorists' reasoning is that the millions of ordinary tourists wouldn't be frightened by the kidnapping of famous people, but they would be discouraged by the random abduction of some of their own number.'

'That's an interesting possibility, Chief,' commented Miranda, 'but would ETA *Militar* abduct all the victims from Torremolinos? There are no reports of disappearances from other resorts.'

'That's a crucial point, Carlos,' admitted Bernal. 'We'll ask Madrid to check all centres for us. It would be best to ring Inspector Ibáñez in Central Records, Paco. You know they've moved him up to the Escorial now, to be with the national police computer they call "Berta"? I don't want to tell the

Anti-Terrorist Group Superintendent about Palencia's other problems here yet, which may not be at all connected.'

'I've been thinking of a very different possibility, Chief,' said Lista quietly.

A shadow passed over Bernal's countenance, making it appear more gloomy and severe than it normally did. 'Yes, Juan, it's at the forefront of my mind, too. We may be dealing with a local psychopath, a serial murderer, and judging by the rapidly increasing frequency of the reported disappearances he may be nearing the climax of his crimes.'

'If it is a case of a serial murderer, Chief,' commented Miranda, who had read a good many books on criminal psychopathy, 'wouldn't one expect there to have been earlier cases at more spaced-out intervals?'

'That's why I asked Palencia this morning to get on to Málaga Records and get them to look back at the reports for the past five years. It would be strange if such a murderer killed five times in ten days without any prior crimes. The psychotic rhythm would be very unusual.'

'Unless the psychopath had moved into the district very recently, Comisario,' commented Palencia.

'Ibáñez should be able to tell us something from the national computer records,' said Bernal. 'We'd better ask him to check all unsolved disappearances of young men for the past five years, just in case some pattern emerges.'

'Isn't this outside our remit, Chief?' asked Navarro.

'I can see that the head of the Anti-Terrorist Group may come to think that,' said Bernal. 'That's why we won't tell him yet. But serious crimes may have been committed on Palencia's patch, and he hasn't got the manpower to cover them as well as look for bombs on the beaches and terrorists in the hotels. Our remit is to help him, and I take that to mean in everything until Madrid orders otherwise. After all, serious crime is our business. Do you all agree?'

They all nodded their assent, and Palencia looked relieved and grateful.

'May I propose a way of proceeding that should cover all eventualities?' said Bernal. 'In the case of four of the missing youths, we have no leads at all, but we shall shortly have photographs of them via Interpol. In the fifth case, that of the missing German youth called Keller, we have the fact of his telephoning home to say he had booked in at the Lido Apartments. Inspector Palencia sent his corporal there to question the manager, but he seems to have drawn a blank. That needs more looking into, and I intend to follow it up. What we want in all five cases is more background information about the way these youths spent their time in Torremolinos. What bars and discothèques did they frequent? Which cheap restaurants did they eat in? Are drugs involved? Or prostitution? I therefore propose that Ángel and Elena should work undercover, booking into any of the lodging-houses frequented by these transient visitors, and there find out what they can by mixing with these young foreigners.'

Ángel looked very happy at this proposal, while Elena reacted more cautiously.

Bernal now looked at Miranda and Palencia. 'I'm afraid the rest of us would look out of place in those surroundings; we'd never blend in. But we can make a start on a *pensión*-to-*pensión* inquiry, armed with the mugshots of the ETA terrorists and of the missing youths. They all must have stayed somewhere. If we mix up the photos of the ten *etarras* and the five youths, it will be less obvious to the reception-clerks and managers what we're looking for.'

'I think that's a terrific plan, Chief,' said Ángel joyfully. 'Elena and I will have a great time.'

'You must on no account put Elena at any unnecessary risk.'

'Don't worry about me, Chief,' said Elena. 'It sounds as though Ángel will be more in the firing line than I, considering what's happened in this case so far.'

After the conference, Ángel and Elena had a quick confab about their assignment.

'If you like, Elena, I'll stroll along San Miguel – that's the main thoroughfare along which everyone staying here has to pass two or three times a day – and see if there are any vacancies in the lodging-houses before it gets dark. There may not be any later on.'

'That's fine, Ángel, but I think we'd better book in individually and make it look as though we're strangers who happen to meet there. In any case we'll want separate rooms.'

'Will we? I thought we'd get a double room to save the Chief's expense account,' said Ángel tongue-in-cheek.

Elena ignored the remark. 'I'm going to need a new wardrobe in any case. These tailor-made things won't do.' She looked critically at Ángel's almost punk-like get-up. 'I suppose I'll have to go to the Indian bazaars and look for some cheap and common things to match your outfit.'

'Cheap? Common? I'll have you know that these slacks and this shirt cost me a bomb in a Madrid boutique in the Calle Gravina. They're the latest fashion, the "in" things!' he retorted indignantly.

'Gravina? From one of those side-streets behind the Café Gijón? They must have seen you coming, Ángel.' She wrinkled her aristocratic nose disdainfully. 'You were robbed.'

'You can take me on a shopping expedition when we get back and pick out some suitable things for me, if we're going to see so much of each other.'

Elena fixed him with an icy stare. 'I'll meet you back here at seven-thirty, or you can ring me to tell me where there's a vacant room.' She strode off without giving him a further glance.

Ángel Gallardo, whom nobody could have guessed was a full-blown inspector in the Brigada Criminal if they had seen him weighed down by a backpack, struggled through the swirling evening crowd of gaily dressed tourists in the Calle de San Miguel and kept his eyes skinned for lodging-houses still announcing vacancies for that night.

The first five *pensiónes* he came to all had the 'Full' notice displayed, and soon he had come to the small square at the bottom of the street above the Windmill restaurant and the start of the steps leading down to the Bajondillo. There were far more tourists climbing the slope than descending at that hour, and some of them had clearly made the effort to dress for dinner, in the sense of having discarded their beach-shorts in favour of lightweight slacks or summer skirts according to their sex.

Ángel's policeman's eye quickly took in the busy scene along the first main slope cut out of the high rock. There were rickety stalls, obviously hastily erected, the owners of which were desultorily proffering for sale handmade paste or carved jewellery, mock crocodile-skin belts and wallets, ghastly cigarette-boxes made of painted shells, and beach-hats with comic and even mildly obscene mottoes printed on them in various European languages. Here and there small groups of holidaymakers stopped to watch young artists struggling to obtain approximate and rapidly sketched likenesses of such unpromising subjects as plump Nordic blondes with sun-reddened cheeks and peeling noses; or they gazed in lazy fascination at child acrobats and prestidigitators, or got embroiled with the furtive cardsharpers standing at tiny collapsible tables who offered the unsuspecting punters the chance of doubling their thousand-peseta notes in all variations of the trick of 'Find the Queen', with their mock-innocent stooges on hand to win the trick on the first three occasions. Ángel wondered why the municipal police hadn't seen these tricksters off long since.

He was now passing the first row of small lodging-houses on the upper section of the Cuesta del Tago and he enquired hopefully at the doorways, but the owners shook their heads and pointed him further down the crowded narrow lane. 'You may get in at one of those pubs. They let out rooms on a nightly basis.'

On reaching the first hairpin turn, Ángel saw a sizeable crowd gathered outside the entrance to a white-painted three-storey building that seemed to have once consisted of a group

83

of the original fishermen's cottages in the days before international tourism had struck this once idyllic village. Easing his way through the crush that almost blocked the footpath, Ángel caught glimpses of a tall, blond, willowy figure clothed in a tight pink dress with a pencil-skirt slit on the right side nearly to the waist, who swayed rather drunkenly to the rhythm of a distorted cassette of an Argentinian tango that emerged from a battery recorder placed on the white-washed doorstep of the house.

'¡Yo soy Lola! – I'm Lola!' sang this extraordinary vision in a slightly husky falsetto. '¡Lola de Linares!'

The crowd that consisted mostly of tipsy young foreigners clapped encouragement and shouted 'Olé' to urge the artiste to greater efforts. Behind her on the wall of the house, Ángel could now see a promising sign: 'ZIMMER - CHAMBRES - ROOMS'; every important language except his own, he noticed. Just then a perspiring, balding, grotesquely obese, middle-aged man carrying a broomstick appeared at the doorway of the establishment and brandished it in a threatening manner at the *bailarina*.

'Be off with you! I've told you before not to create a scandal outside my door!' He kicked the cassette-player off his doorstep, and the tinny music ground to a sudden halt.

The crowd started to boo in disapproval as Lola from Linares stooped precariously on her stiletto heels to recover the machine and examine its controls anxiously. '¡Hijo de puta! You've ruined it!'

Some of the young foreigners in the throng, grasping the meaning of her words and gestures, began to throw coins and notes at Lola's feet. 'Buy yourself another one, love! Give us another number!'

The fat proprietor stood his ground until Lola tiredly gathered her belongings and started to totter up the hill. Ángel pushed his way to the lodging-keeper's side.

'Have you got any rooms free?'

The stout, nearly bald man looked him up and down, then nodded.

'Just two left. You can come and inspect them and take your pick.'

After the crowd had dispersed, Ángel followed the man through the cool *zaguán* – a blue-and-white-tiled passageway leading to the inner courtyard.

'That *travesti*!' expostulated the fat owner. 'Why does he always choose my front door to give his ridiculous performances? Do you realise that he must make five thousand a day between what he picks up at lunchtime on the terraces of the beach restaurants and in the evenings up in La Nogalera? The police should run him in.'

Having been obliged to step over a large but friendly-looking watchdog that lay across a right-angled turn in the *zaguán*, they emerged into an irregularly shaped patio fragrant with flowering plants that spilled from terracotta pots surrounding a very tall date-palm, the fronds of which reached high above the red pantiles of the roofs. Ángel saw that there were at least three exterior tiled staircases leading to separate dwellings and realised that this lodging-house had been created out of a court of houses of different styles and periods. All had been given a certain unity by the generous application of whitewash and Mauresque tiles.

As he turned towards the side of the yard that formed an attractive balcony over the lower rooftops of the Bajondillo with the sea beyond, Ángel was amused at seeing a young man lying prone across the stone surround of a well, with his shorts pulled down to his ankles while a very plump red-faced woman in her sixties vigorously worked a thick white ointment into his buttocks with the palms of her hands.

'What on earth are you doing, Anna?' shouted the stout proprietor in alarm. 'Are you crazy? What will people think?'

'Don't worry, Albert. The sun has burnt him badly. He has been to the nudist beach by the golf-course. He must have ointment.'

Ángel noticed the strong foreign – perhaps German – flavour of the woman's Spanish, though she spoke it with great fluency, while he took the old man's accent to be Catalan.

'Do it in the kitchen, then, not out here where everyone can see!' He gestured to Ángel. 'Come. We have two rooms vacant on this staircase over our living-quarters.'

When Navarro got the message from Madrid that Doctor Peláez had boarded the Iberia evening flight to Málaga, Bernal decided to go in person to Rompedizo airport to meet him. As the police driver took him north-eastwards along the main N340 they soon ran into a long queue of vehicles.

'It's the Guardia Civil control, Superintendent. Shall I try using the blue oscillator on the roof and the siren? We might make it along the hard shoulder.'

Bernal consulted his Bulova watch. 'We've still got half an hour. Take your time.'

He lit up a Káiser and took out a red-covered file from his attaché case. Pulling slowly on the black tobacco, he began to reread the local police surgeon's autopsy report on the young policeman, which he had brought along to hand over to Peláez. He noticed some loose sheets attached to the back of the typewritten folios with a paper-clip. Turning at once to these, he saw they were a copy of the periodic police medical reports on the deceased officer. Bernal noted that the man had always enjoyed perfect health, with totally normal blood-pressure and pulse readings, and had been something of an amateur sportsman, having played tennis and squash and the occasional game of football for the Málaga police team.

Bernal found it increasingly difficult to believe that such a person could have suffered a sudden cerebral haemorrhage. The Málaga pathologist had diligently examined the vagus nerve and dissected out the larynx for signs of abrasion or injury which could indicate death by vagal inhibition, but had found nothing. That method of delivering a blow with the edge of the hand, Bernal knew, was commonly taught in unarmed-combat classes for use during hostilities against enemy sentries, since it had the advantage of causing instant and silent death, but this could not be effected without leaving damage to the hyoid or thyroid bones or the voice-box itself – signs that any reasonably competent pathologist could hardly miss. Bernal still nursed the hope that Doctor Peláez, with his longer and wider experience, would spot something amiss with the local man's findings.

It was getting quite dark as their car approached the checkpoint, and when the Civil Guard caught sight of Bernal's warrant-card and the gold-star badge of a *comisario de primera*, he saluted sharply and waved them to proceed, but Bernal asked to speak to the officer in charge, who came over to them at once, holding an eager-looking dog on a lead.

'Have you come across anything suspicious, Lieutenant?'

The officer shook his head. 'Not so far, Superintendent.'

'Please remember that we want you not only to look out for the *etarras* from the police photos but also to be on the watch for portable radio transmitters, as well as explosives.'

'We're checking all the boot compartments, in addition to the interior of the vehicles, Comisario. And this Labrador is trained to sniff out even tiny traces of most types of explosive.'

'Please warn your men that these terrorists will be well armed and that they may shoot to kill as soon as they think they've been spotted. They're dangerous fanatics.'

'I'll tell them, sir.'

Inspector Ángel Gallardo looked into the first room shown him by the perspiring proprietor and saw that it had a row of small windows with half-closed yellow curtains that overlooked the main patio of the establishment. It contained little more than two single beds with brass-railed headposts, a large rickety wardrobe, and a primitive-looking handbasin standing precariously on the uneven black-and-white-tiled floor.

'How much is this one? It's a double, isn't it?'

'Yes, but you can have it for eight hundred a night; money in advance. How many nights are you thinking of staying?'

'About a week to ten days, I expect. Can I see the other room?'

'This way.'

The corpulent lodging-keeper wheezed loudly as he led Ángel along a dark twisting corridor with sloping floors and occasional unexpected steps towards the front of the building.

'There are two bathrooms on this floor.' He pushed at the latch of an ancient black-painted door which creaked open to reveal a young girl, naked to the waist, who was busy dyeing her hair to a Titian shade, to judge by the liquid dripping from it into the chipped sink.

'Hey! Do you mind?'

'Sorry, my dear,' simpered the old man, beaming lasciviously. 'You should have bolted the door.'

'You bloody well know it won't lock, you old goat!'

He pulled the door shut with a bang and gestured to Ángel to follow him down three steps to a corridor that went off at a right angle.

'Here's the other room. It's a bit dearer – one thousand one hundred a night – but it's got a wonderful view!'

Ángel could see that it also had the disadvantage of being a couple of metres from the noisy lane leading down to the Bajondillo. At that moment the room looked attractive, as though from a tourist brochure, since it was flooded with the red sunset-light and offered a distant view of the waves breaking on the rocks at the Punta de Torremolinos with La Roca and the castle romantically *contre-jour*. Moving to lean out of the window, Ángel saw that it also provided an excellent observation-post.

'I'll take the cheaper one.'

The man nodded; it was all that he had expected of this pleasant but clearly impoverished compatriot. 'That'll be five thousand six hundred for a week in advance.'

Ángel shelled out the notes with obvious reluctance. 'Can I have a receipt?'

'Come down to the office afterwards where it will be ready for you.'

'Is there a public phone?'

'Not here. We've got a private line which could be used in an emergency, but we haven't got a meter, you see, to let all the guests use it whenever they want. But there's one across the lane in the Red Lion, and a phone-box at the bottom of the hill.'

Ángel returned to the first room and dumped his haversack on the nearer bed. He was startled to see two enormous cockroaches fleeing in terror from under it. OK, he sighed, so it was going to be that sort of a dump. He should have been expecting them in such an old building. He'd buy some insecticide in the general store he had seen beyond the second pub, the Britannia.

He locked the door of his room and started down the outside staircase. On the balcony on the other side of the patio he was delighted to catch a glimpse of two Scandinavian blondes sitting ostensibly naked in the doorway of their room. He blew them kisses and shouted in Spanish: 'Aren't you going to invite me up for a drink, girls?'

'You speak English?' One of them got up without any embarrassment, and he could see she was wearing the briefest of monokinis.

'We have drink with you later. We cooling off now.'

Ángel remembered enough of his ill-learned English to understand and to reply. 'I can see that, sweeties. You want a rub down in the shower?'

'Hah! Only one shower-house, see?' They pointed down at the palm tree. 'Long line to get in; you wait many minutes.'

Ángel now noticed near the wall at the far end of the patio a queue of seven or eight young people of different nationalities and in various stages of undress who clutched towels, bars of soap and bottles of shampoo, while he could hear a persistent hiss of water coming from the open window of the bath-house.

'Hot only for one hour,' added one of the Scandinavian girls. 'You hurry.'

'I will; do not worry. Don't go cold on me.'

Ángel rapidly concluded that there were going to be compensations for the cockroaches in this strange establishment after all. In the *zaguán* he stopped to make friends with the old St Bernard dog, who sniffed at him suspiciously but then turned over on its side and licked the back of Ángel's hand.

'What's your name, eh, doggy? I must find out. You could come in handy one of these dark nights.'

As he passed the office-window, the red-faced landlady, who was sewing up a tear in a sheet, waved at him gaily. He crossed the busy lane and entered the Red Lion, which was crammed with young tourists drinking pints of imported English beer and yelling as though they were quarrelling above the noise of a Donna Summer record turned up to maximum volume.

Seeing the telephone in the corner beyond the bar, Ángel fought his way to it, placed two *duro* coins on the metal slide and dialled the number of the Hotel Paraíso. He placed his forefinger in his right ear in order to hear the receptionist in his left as he asked for Elena's room.

'You've bought all you needed?'

'Yes, Ángel. Where are you?'

'Not far away – just down the lane towards the Bajondillo. It's after the first major turn in the cliff-path. The Casa España; they've still got one room left, if you hurry. It's got a wonderful view of the bay.'

'OK. I'll be there in ten minutes.'

Ángel forced his way to the bar having decided he'd try the English beer; he was soon shocked at the price. A *caña* of Águila lager in his Madrid haunts only cost twenty-five pesetas, but a glass three times as large of this imported beer cost 300 here. In the midst of this lively and mainly incomprehensible crowd, he began to wish he had been more assiduous in his attendance at the evening classes at the British Institute in the Calle de Almagro, but he had hated having to learn the verb-forms, which seemed to be the key to everything. Nevertheless, with his outstanding capacity for gesture and mimicry, he usually got by with great aplomb. Soon he was in confused but animated conversation with his neighbour at the bar, a red-haired Irishman.

'I'm Jimmy. Where're you from, Angel?'

'Madrid. I'm spending ten days here.'

'Where are you staying?' Ángel pointed at the Casa España. 'What a coincidence! So am I. Did you see those Swedish girls, Angel?' He pronounced 'Angel' as though it were an English word, with a palatal g.

'They often walk about with no clothes?'

'Most of the time, but they're always high on smack.'

' "Smack"? What "smack"?'

'I don't know what you call it in Spain. It's a mixture of coke and junk. They also get angel dust now and then.' He nudged Ángel knowingly. 'Hey, you should try it, since it's named after you! They heat it up on tinfoil and sniff it.'

'But where you buy it, Jimmy?'

Jimmy looked around cautiously. 'Here, there, anywhere. A lot of those Moroccans sell it. I think they bring it in through Algeciras. There's plenty of grass, too, very cheap here on the coast.'

As Jimmy chatted on, behind him through the small-paned windows Ángel watched out for Elena's arrival. At first he failed to recognise her, so well had she adapted her appearance to the surroundings. Having had her brown hair highlighted with bleach and its style completely changed, she had put on pink Bermuda shorts and a tank top with large-framed sunglasses to match. She was weighed down with a heavy rucksack. Ángel observed her hesitating opposite the 'ROOMS VACANT' sign outside the Casa España, resting her burden on the pavement, but soon she entered that curious establishment. He decided to give her ten minutes to settle in.

After Superintendent Bernal had talked to the Civil Guard senior officer in charge at Rompedizo airport, the police car was allowed to drive through the barrier and pull up on the edge of the tarmac in front of the national flights terminal. He had been informed that the evening Iberia flight from Madrid had left only five minutes late. He was amazed to see the number of foreign airliners parked outside the international terminal: a plane seemed to take off or land every six or seven minutes.

91

Soon he saw a Boeing 727 coming in low from the sea, almost pausing as it touched down at the head of the main runway. Its jets roared as they were thrust into reverse. The gleaming craft braked quite sharply, then taxied rapidly off the runway towards them. When the engines were cut, Bernal got out of the car and strolled towards the movable stairway run out by the ground crew. As the first-class passengers began to descend, he at once spotted Doctor Peláez's bald pate and thick pebble-lensed glasses shining under the amber arc-lamps which had now been switched on. The pathologist waved a cheery greeting and then slapped Bernal heavily on the back.

'Well done, Luis! You've got me out of having to accompany my wife to Santander. Where's the body?'

'Now, take your time, Peláez. We've booked you into the best hotel in Málaga. I'll take you there first to check in, then we'll have a spot of dinner and discuss the case. You can cut up the body tomorrow. It won't run away.'

'You know I like to have them as fresh as possible. And untouched by other hands first. I suppose this one's been hacked about as usual?'

' 'Fraid so, but the local chappie can't tell us the cause of death.'

'Ha! It will have been worth the journey, then. Perhaps another one for the next volume of my casebook. You've heard I'm publishing all my interesting cases in chronological order now?'

'I've read all the publicity in the press. I bet they're selling like hot cakes. How much have you been paid?'

'It's a state secret, but not much so far. Now tell me what's happening here.'

Ángel decided he'd given Elena enough time to negotiate for the room, so he sauntered back to the boarding-house with the irrepressible Jimmy.

'Shall we go out and pull some birds later, Angel?'

Very puzzled by this vulgar English expression, Ángel none the less agreed to anything. Pull some birds? Surely the red-haired fellow couldn't be intending to go hunting in the dark. Ángel began to suspect that the prey Jimmy had in mind must be human.

When they entered the Casa España and found their passage impeded by the St Bernard, Jimmy straddled the animal and patted its head.

'Come on, you old softie. Let us by.'

'What its name, Jimmy?'

'Remmy, I think.' The great beast lifted up its front paws to lick Jimmy's face and almost knocked him to the floor.

Remmy? Ángel wondered. Ah, he got it in one. Rémy Martin, the Cognac. The patio was now empty, all the *inquilinos* having apparently showered themselves at the reglamentary time. When they ascended the outside staircase, he discovered that Jimmy's room was next to the bathroom he had seen earlier.

'Did you see the French bint, Angel, the one who's always changing the colour of her hair? The one from upstairs? She's here on her own. Most of them come in pairs, one ugly and one good-looking. Try having it off with her later.'

Ángel nodded agreeably and gave a wave meant to indicate temporary dismissal. He entered his room cautiously, sensing an intruder as soon as he sniffed the air. Instead of switching the light on, he stood behind the half-open door for a few moments, watching the yellow curtains swaying in the light off-shore breeze. When his eyes had grown more accustomed to the dimness, he caught a glimpse of a dark shape between the curtains at the far end of the room.

'Psst! You want some grass or *chocolate*?' hissed a foreign voice.

Ángel switched on the light and closed the door. The large Berber face of the Moroccan he had seen in the patio earlier grinned at him from the window. Ángel strolled over.

'How much?'

'Very cheap. A *porro* will cost you two hundred.'

'OK . Give me a couple.' Ángel took the ill-made cigarettes and sniffed them.

'It's good stuff, from Ceuta. Whenever you want anything, I'm along there in chalet number five.'

Ángel paid him the money, and watched as the huge dark figure slipped with surprising agility across the patio and into the shadow of the palm-fronds. Ángel leant out to see how the intruder had managed to reach the window. At once he saw another staircase he hadn't known about before which led presumably to the rooftop where, according to Jimmy, the now Titian-haired French girl had her quarters. He would have to explore this extraordinary warren more thoroughly in daylight.

Now he locked the end windows securely and drew all the curtains. He turned to his rucksack and examined the locks; they hadn't been forced. He took out his keys and unrolled the pack: all his special police equipment was still intact, including his service pistol and radio transceiver. It looked as though the Moroccan drug-pusher hadn't actually climbed into his room; perhaps he had been waiting in the shadows and had seen Jimmy and him coming in.

Ángel opened the door again to peep out; he paused for a minute or two to listen. The Swedish girls opposite hadn't bothered to draw the curtain across the glass double-doors of their room, and he could see that they were minimally dressing to go out. He closed his door silently and moved down the corridor towards the room Elena must have taken. He stopped on the landing outside the bathroom, the door of which was ajar. He put his head in and found no one, but he could hear the noise of music and shouting from the pub across the lane.

He re-emerged to hear loud whispering from Jimmy's room, and an occasional groan. At first eavesdropping, then squinting through the keyhole, he could see the large curly-headed Moroccan holding down Jimmy's head over the table, over which a cloud of thin white smoke hung. So the Irishman was into smack or some such drug. At all events it should keep him quiet for a bit.

Ángel edged his way along the turn in the corridor to Elena's room and tapped gently on the door. He could see no cracks of light showing. His colleague opened the door a centimetre and whispered: 'Who is it?'

'You should have asked that before opening the door, you know. You've forgotten all your training.'

'No, I haven't.' She dug him in the ribs with the butt of her service revolver. 'See?'

'OK, I give in.' He put his hands up in mock surrender. 'Why are you in the dark?'

'Shhh! Don't talk so loud. Come over to the left side of the window,' she ordered mysteriously.

Puzzled, Ángel followed her across the darkened room. Standing behind her, with the tantalising scent of her Parisian perfume in his nostrils, he looked beyond the narrow lane to the rooftops that stretched away towards the cliff. His keen ears caught the sound of high-pitched howls and loud purrs, and soon he could descry a number of cats swirling excitedly on the tiles.

'So what? It's just a pack of stray cats.'

'Shhh! Not so loud!' Elena admonished. 'It's not them; it's the man who's feeding them.'

'Where?'

'Under the overhang of the roof to the right, below the railings,' she breathed.

At first Ángel managed only to spot an arm emerging from the shadows, throwing titbits to the screeching and fighting cats. He shrugged: 'Just a fellow who feeds the strays.'

They watched for two or three more minutes, but the man still didn't emerge into the light afforded by the electric lanterns mounted along the lane. Suddenly the wild-cats turned away from the source of their bounty and began to squabble among themselves.

'He's gone,' said Elena in surprise. 'How did he get away without our seeing him?'

'There must be a way down to the rocks from the other side.' Ángel drew the curtains and went to switch on the light. 'Why all the mystery, then? He was only an animal crank.'

'I'm not sure why he caught my attention when he came up the lane among so many tourists; perhaps because he looked

95

so different – so menacing.' She shivered suddenly. 'It was the way he looked up at this window—'

'You're imagining things! He was just an eccentric cat-lover. It's a smashing room you've got, isn't it?'

'You've chosen a fine place, I must say,' she said accusingly. 'Did you bring any insecticide?'

'Oh Lord, I forgot to buy it. I was intending to until I met Jimmy. Why, have you found any bugs?'

'Bugs! This old place is crawling with cockroaches, and the loo is infested with giant ants, or hadn't you noticed? And I see you've given me the poorer of the two vacant rooms.'

'Not at all! This one is much more expensive than my interior one.'

'And noisier and dirtier. I shan't sleep a wink and I'll have to go back every morning to the Paraíso to disinfest myself and catch up on some sleep.'

'Hey, that wasn't in the Chief's plans for us. Anyway, you've got a grandstand view of all the inhabitants of the town who have to pass here on their way to the beach. But tell me about this mysterious cat-lover,' said Ángel, mostly to change the subject, though he was still much intrigued by her nervous reaction.

'Oh, it's probably not important. It was just the horrible look on the man's face. I was watching out for you, with the light switched off, after I'd been on the bug-hunt under the bed, when I saw him coming up the lane carrying two bulging plastic bags. He looked so utterly out of place, but that wasn't what caught my attention.'

'What did, then?'

'It was the very furtive way he glanced up and down the cliff-path before jumping over the railings on to the roof over there.'

'Nothing very odd about that, is there? Of course he shouldn't go walking about on other people's tiles, but fanatical pet-lovers are all dotty.'

'It was the strange expression on his face under the lantern.' Elena gave an involuntary shiver. 'It was' – she hesitated – 'an expression of pure evil.'

'Impure, you mean,' laughed Ángel. 'You're sure he didn't see you?'

'I don't think so. I drew back inside the window-frame, but I could feel his wickedness as though a malediction emanated from him.' She pulled a light jacket round her shoulders. 'But I know you'll say I'm being silly, so forget it; it's nothing to do with our investigation.'

After ten minutes had passed, the tall stranger re-emerged from behind the chimney-pots and looked up at the lodging-house opposite. He saw a light on now and the pink-flowered curtains drawn. On them he could see the silhouettes of a man and the woman he had seen earlier. Nosy bastards! Why didn't they get on with their adulteries and leave him alone? His mangy cats rubbed themselves affectionately against his trouser-legs as he moved lightly across the tiles; he saw they had torn the plastic bags in which he had wrapped the offal into a thousand shreds. On reaching the lane, he glanced quickly to right and left and, seeing no one, he vaulted the railings and made for the shadows further up the path, whistling softly to himself.

Having had an early dinner with Peláez in his luxurious hotel, Bernal left him the initial forensic report on the dead police-man to study overnight. He had filled the famous pathologist in on the matter of the bomb explosions and on the case of the missing foreign youths.

Bernal now told the official driver to take him to the Gobierno Civil building in the Plaza de la Aduana. There he found the Chief of Police still in his office after 10 p.m. surrounded by piles of papers and harassed minions.

'Ah, Comisario. Nothing has happened in Torremolinos, has it?'

'Not as far as I know. I've just brought Doctor Peláez the pathologist from the airport. I've asked him to perform a second autopsy on Palencia's man.'

'A good idea. We must get to the bottom of it.' He waved a paper at Bernal. 'We've just had our first explosion.' He sounded almost proud of it. 'At Benalmádena, west of you. It went off on the promenade in the middle of the evening *paseo*.'

'Were there any casualties?'

'Only a lot of earth and bits of concrete sprayed over the people eating on the restaurant terraces. The bomb was buried in a large jardinière built round a palm tree by the Parks Department.'

'So it wasn't buried in the sand on the beach like the other ones in other provinces,' commented Bernal worriedly. 'They seem to be changing their tactics.'

'That's exactly what I was thinking. But ours,' he said proprietorially, 'consisted of a very small charge, clearly meant to frighten rather than to kill. The army experts are at the scene now.'

'Have they found out how it was set off?' asked Bernal. 'The other bombs seem to have been exploded by remote control so that the *etarras* could observe the scene and see who was passing at the time. But this Benalmádena bomb seems to have been indiscriminate in its effects.'

'And it makes it impossible for us to search every bit of garden outside all the thousands of hotels, apartments and restaurants in the province. It's really a nightmare.'

'Have the Civil Guard road-blocks come up with anything?'

'Nothing at all, except for a few local villains we've been after for quite a while.'

'Well, it's an ill wind. . . .'

'My sentiments exactly,' said the police chief. 'I comfort myself with the old proverb: "A río revuelto, ganancia de pescadores." '

'The river along this coast is stirred up enough for any number of fishermen to profit from it,' commented Bernal. 'We'll keep in touch, Chief. I'm returning to Torremolinos now.'

It was almost 10.30 p.m. when the police car approached the interchange to the north-east of Torremolinos. On a sudden impulse Bernal instructed the driver to take him

98

down the Avenida del Lido. 'Stop at the apartments at the Lido Square.'

The Apartamentos del Lido seemed pretty well deserted at that hour, and Bernal shivered slightly in the strong breeze as he entered the garden. To the right he saw a light in the office and made for it. The night porter, who turned out to be a dark-haired Andalusian with a pronounced squint in his right eye, was watching on a portable television set the 'Ahí te quiero ver' chat-show presented by the lively Catalan actress Rosa María Sardá.

'Don't switch it off,' said Bernal, showing his Comisario's badge, 'just turn the sound down. Now, tell me about this German youth who booked a room here last Friday night.' He slapped the Interpol photo on to the desk.

'But I never saw him, Superintendent! I told the corporal who came round to my house.'

'But the youth phoned home and told his family he had booked in here. How do you explain that?'

The porter flushed as Bernal fixed him with sharply inquisitorial eyes. 'He made a mistake! He never came here when I was on duty.'

'Tell me about room fourteen. Is it occupied tonight?'

'No, sir.'

'Get the key, then, and we'll go and take a look.'

With obvious reluctance, the man got the key, which was attached to a green-and-white plastic tag, from a board on the wall and led Bernal out across the dark lawn.

'It's right next to the bar of the restaurant.'

The sound of flamenco dancing got louder as they approached the chalet, the front of which consisted of a small veranda divided from its neighbour by a two-metre wooden partition painted green. Beyond the two white-painted chairs on the minuscule patio was a wooden door, split horizontally in the manner of the door of a stable, set between two large windows that were screened by dirty-looking net curtains. Inside, the only furniture consisted of a double bed and a built-in wardrobe and dressing-table. At the back a glass door led into a windowless bathroom, which Bernal inspected carefully with a torch for signs of bloodstains.

'Has this room been let out in the past few days?'

'No, sir. Not since last Friday.'

The porter bit his tongue, but Bernal gave no sign that he had noticed the slip. He began to open the drawers and cupboards and shone his torch into them.

'You can go back to the office and wait. I'll be some time here.'

When Ángel returned to his room, after arranging to contrive to bump into Elena in the presence of other guests as though meeting her for the first time, he came upon Jimmy knocking at his door, looking none the worse for wear.

'What say we go for a fling up in the main square, Angel?'

'OK.'

Just then the French girl came tottering on the highest of high heels down the farther staircase, hobbled by a very tight, black, simulated-leather skirt, and met them in the patio.

'You coming out with us?' Jimmy asked her. Ángel noted that his pupils were very dilated and that he showed every sign of being high.

'I not sure.' The girl looked at them doubtfully. 'With two of you. . . .'

At that moment Elena made a spectacular appearance down the central staircase, wearing a white Indian crêpe dress with flounced skirt and a sprig of artificial white camellias in her newly tinted hair.

Jimmy made a wolf-whistle. 'Say, look at that. Do you know her?'

'I never seen her before,' said Ángel, turning to smile encouragingly at the French girl who began to flutter her long false eyelashes at him after catching a glimpse of the competition. 'Comment vous appelez-vous?' At least he could remember one phrase of French.

'Paulette. Je suis de Marseille. Et vous?'

'Ángel.'

'Comment? C'est un ange, n'est-ce-pas?'

'That is right – an angel, that's me. I behave myself always.'

Paulette stole a glance at her potential rival, Elena, who at that moment was being fawned upon by the red-haired Irishman at the foot of the stairs, and she made a decision. 'OK, I come out with you.'

'This is Helena, Angel. She says she'll come with us, too.'

With a straight face Ángel shook hands politely with his fellow-inspector, who looked sharply at the French girl.

'This is great,' said Jimmy jubilantly. 'A foursome. We'll hit all the high spots tonight.'

'Something to eat first?' asked Elena – in quite respectable English, thought Ángel enviously.

'Yeah, we'll go up to the Vaca Sentada. You know it? "The Sitting Cow"? We'll have us some rump-steaks there.'

Elena shuddered slightly, but took Jimmy's proffered arm, while Ángel took that of the Marseillaise, who certainly looked the part.

When the police car pulled out of the Lido Square, Bernal asked the driver to take him to an address on the outskirts of town. After they had crossed the N340 and climbed into the barren hills above, Bernal could see the skeletal outlines of many half-constructed apartment-blocks looming up in the dark between the garish lights of Torremolinos and the headlights of the vehicles travelling at speed along the bypass on the higher ground.

Entering a street that had no tarmac surface or lighting, the driver drew up at the entrance of one of the jerry-built apartment-houses. 'This is it, sir.'

'Come in with me, will you? I want to put on a bit of a show.'

At Bernal's peremptory ring, the door of the second-floor apartment was opened by a frightened-looking woman who was clearly trying to put four children to bed. Bernal showed his badge and entered with the uniformed man.

'You are the wife of the night porter at the Lido Apartments?'

'Yes, sir, I am.' She wiped her dry hands nervously on her apron.

'You also work there as a chambermaid and do the laundry?'

'Some of it, sir.' She pointed at the sheets hanging on the balcony outside.

'Now, I must inform you that your husband has confessed everything to me.' He pulled out the Interpol photo of Keller, the German youth. 'You changed the sheets in room fourteen after this youth disappeared, didn't you? Where did you hide his belongings?' He looked pointedly around the room, while the woman began to wail and the children hid behind the settee.

'Nowhere, sir, I swear I didn't. I never saw them – nor him, neither.'

'But your husband took his money all right, didn't he? For two nights, wasn't it, in the hope the manager wouldn't find out?'

'Oh, you wouldn't tell the manager, would you, sir? We'll both lose our jobs and be ruined!' She began to sob.

'Worse things will happen to you if you don't tell me everything now, do you understand? You'll have to accompany us to the station for questioning.'

'Oh God, no. Please don't take me away. What will become of the children?'

'You should have thought of that before aiding and abetting a fraud, or was it a murder?'

She blanched and gasped: 'Murder? He was murdered?' She crossed herself hastily. 'We did nothing to him, nothing, neither my husband nor me. I never even saw him.'

'Tell me everything.' She began to shake, so Bernal took her gently by the arm and led her to a battered easy-chair. He sat down on the arm of it alongside her.

'When my husband came home on Saturday morning, he told me to be sure to do room fourteen myself that day, which was the manager's day off, and on the next day – Sunday

102

– in order to change the sheets and towels first thing and clean the room before the boss came back on duty. There's only that gardening lad there at the weekend and he never notices anything.'

'Wouldn't he notice the room-key missing from the board?'

She looked cunning for a moment. 'All the boarders keep their keys with them, and I have a master-key, like the one in the manager's office. But there were two guest's keys for room fourteen, because in the past people had gone off with the key when checking out and only once bothered to send it back.'

'So your husband kept the original key to room fourteen without telling the manager it had been returned?'

She nodded. 'My husband gave one to the foreign youth who booked in on Friday night, but the chap never came back, you see. On Saturday morning I found the bed hadn't been slept in and the room hadn't been used.'

'What about his luggage?'

'There was nothing, I swear to you by all the saints. He must have taken off the night before with all his belongings.'

'Yet your husband pocketed the two thousand four hundred pesetas he had paid for the two nights in advance.' She nodded and bent her head in shame. 'But why would anyone pay that much money and go away again?'

'I don't know,' she wailed. 'We thought he'd gone off to a different place along the coast, or even that he'd had to go home unexpectedly.'

'So he left nothing, nothing at all in room fourteen?'

'I didn't find anything. He hadn't even used the bathroom.'

'But he took something away with him, didn't he?' mused Bernal.

'There was nothing missing.'

'The other room-key, woman, he took that.'

'Yes,' she admitted, 'I suppose he must have done.'

'And did it have the same engraved plastic tag as the others I saw on the board?'

'Yes, sir, they're all the same. The guests aren't expected to hand them in whenever they go out. They keep them for their whole stay.'

'You and your husband must report early tomorrow morning to Inspector Palencia in the *comisaría* in the Plaza de Andalucía and make full depositions, you understand?'

'But you won't tell the manager of the apartments, will you? Otherwise we'll be out on our necks.'

'We'll say nothing to your employer for the time being.'

On the way down the stairs Bernal glanced at the uniformed man quizzically. 'I hope you didn't think I was too hard on her, but it saved time and she'll feel better for having made a clean breast of it.'

'You did it beautifully, sir. You got her to sing like a bird.'

'Will you take me to the Hotel Paraíso for a moment? Then you can drive me back to Cabo Pino and call it a day. I'm sorry it's been such a long one for you.'

'It's been worse for you, Comisario. You ought to try to get a good night's rest.'

Bernal found Navarro still at work in the office. 'The others have knocked off, I suppose, Paco? It's very late.'

'Lista and Miranda have made a good start on the house-to-house inquiry, Chief, but no one has recognised any of the people in the mugshots yet. Ángel and Elena are still at work – if you can call it work. They've put up at the Casa España, in the lane just below this hotel. Ángel has just rung in to report. He says there's an active drugs scene here.'

'It's a very long shot to expect them to find out anything about the missing youths. You should get some rest, Paco. I just want to go down to the hall before I leave. Did Inspector Ibáñez of Central Records get back to you?'

'Not yet, Chief.'

Bernal went down to the lobby and entered the public phone-box to ring Consuelo.

'Luis? Where on earth have you been until now? Thank goodness my sister-in-law has decided to stay on for another week, or I'd have been all on my own. I thought this was to be a really relaxing holiday for us both!'

'I'm very sorry, love. There have been a number of explosions in other provinces, and a small one here in Benalmádena.'

'You don't need to tell me. We've had alarms and excursions all day long on the beach here, what with the Civil Guard and army experts investigating every tin can the children dig up in the sand.'

'But you haven't had a bomb going off, have you? You really shouldn't go too near the beach or the promenade, Chelo.'

'Don't worry. I haven't. You know how the sun gives me freckles. I've been watching it all from the balcony, while the next-door neighbour keeps me informed via the bush telegraph.'

'Your sister-in-law didn't take the children down there, did she?'

'No. They opted for a day out at Tivoli World – you know, that funfair place at Arroyo de la Miel.'

'I'll be with you in under half an hour. There shouldn't be too much traffic now. Hasta luego.'

When Bernal returned to the office to bid goodnight to Navarro, he found him on the phone, waving to him excitedly. Holding his palm across the mouthpiece, he asked: 'Shall I say you've gone, Chief?'

Bernal nodded. Navarro finished the conversation, and turned to his chief. 'It was Palencia, *jefe*. There's been another death; a body found at the back of the Parador de Golf. It's a Civil Guard. Palencia was just leaving to go down there and consult with the Civil Guard top brass.'

'A Civil Guard? But what was he doing on his own? Where was his colleague? Those *parejas* are inseparable always.'

'They were searching the grounds after the concierge had phoned for them. Somebody had spotted intruders up to no good on the eighteenth tee. While the Guards were taking a recce, one of them went back into the hotel to use the facilities, and when he got back he found his colleague dead on the ground. Will you be going down there, Chief?'

'Not on your life. The Guardia Civil will be jealous of their own and wouldn't welcome any interference from us. How was he killed?'

'That's the mysterious thing, Chief. There's not a mark on the body, as far as they can see.'

At 4.55 a.m. on Wednesday, 4 August, Inspector Ángel Gallardo awoke with a start and a heavy head. On the flat roof above him he heard running footsteps punctuated by terrible screams. He groaned as he felt for his service pistol and crept silently to the end window. He caught sight of a tall dark figure running down the outer staircase past his head and watched it leap over the retaining wall and disappear into the night. The loud screams continued in a decelerating but hysterical rhythm, and lights began to go on in the windows opposite. Even Rémy was moved to amble into the main patio where it gave a few token gruff barks.

From the kitchen door below Ángel there emerged the pyjama'd obese figure of the proprietor brandishing a broom, together with his wife dressed in outsize night-attire and clutching a frying-pan; they both looked anxiously up the stairs towards the source of the screams but made no attempt to investigate.

'Do not worry. We have sent for the police,' announced the proprietor to no one in particular.

A jeep could be heard ascending the narrow lane of the Cuesta del Tago and soon it screeched to a halt outside. Two beige-and-brown-uniformed national policemen marched up to the wrought-iron gate in the *zaguán*, which the owner hurried to unlock for them. The St Bernard took mild offence at this official intrusion into his territory and had to be restrained by Anna, who temporarily confined him to the bath-house, from the window of which he peered mournfully out.

Albert pointed quite unnecessarily to the source of the rhythmic screams on the flat roof: 'It's that French girl in number seven.'

The policemen lit powerful flashlights and went up two steps at a time. Soon the screams subsided into loud sobs, and after five minutes had passed the agents descended once more and called the owner's wife to go up. They now began knocking on each door in turn to ask questions. Ángel opened his door and met one of them in the corridor.

'What's up, Officer?'

'It's the French girl upstairs. She claims that a man entered her room by the balcony from the street and tried to rape her. Your room is immediately below hers. Didn't you hear something?'

'I'm afraid not. I was asleep. In fact I accompanied her home with another girl at about four a.m. – we'd been to a discothèque. Elena's room is along this corridor. Do you want me to go up and talk to Paulette?'

'Better not, sir. The owner's wife is trying to calm her and is arranging for her to spend the rest of the night in their quarters downstairs.'

'I should go and see if Elena is all right,' said Ángel worriedly.

'I'll come with you, sir.'

They knocked on Elena's door, and she at once asked who was there. Ángel hoped she wouldn't wave her service revolver at the policeman. She opened the door dressed in a very fetching bathrobe and asked what was wrong.

'Did you hear or see anything about ten minutes ago, señorita?' the policeman asked.

'Before the screams, you mean? No, nothing. I was fast asleep. What's happened?'

'It's Paulette,' explained Ángel hurriedly. 'She says someone shinned up from the street and attempted to rape her.'

'But that's impossible, surely!' exclaimed Elena. 'She's on the second floor, isn't she? Come and see for yourselves from my balcony the height any intruder would have to climb, and there don't seem to be any handholds. He would have to be as agile as Spring-Heeled Jack!'

The policeman and Ángel leant out to inspect the outside wall and admitted she was probably right.

'My colleague is trying to get a description of her attacker, but she speaks virtually no Spanish. The proprietor is attempting to interpret for her. The intruder certainly tore her nightdress and bruised her lip in the struggle, and she must have scratched him, to judge by the scraps of skin caught under her fingernails. Well, I mustn't keep you up any longer, señores. Muy buenas noches.'

When he had gone, Ángel shut the door and sat down on the only chair in the room. 'Phew! That was a close shave. I thought he'd ask for our *carnets* and so make us blow our cover. What a good thing the Chief kept us out of the *comisaría* here right from the start, or he'd have recognised us, most likely.'

'What on earth happened to Paulette?'

'There certainly was an intruder, because I saw him slip over the wall and disappear into the garden of that house where that lad practises the trumpet all day long.'

'She was very drunk when we left the disco,' said Elena, 'so she probably wasn't in much of a state to defend herself.' She thought for a moment. 'I suppose she could have met someone here, after we got back, and invited him up to her room, and then changed her mind and kicked up a fuss.'

'You're quite right about the improbability of anyone climbing up to her balcony from the street,' said Ángel, 'but I don't think she would have invited anyone up there. I discovered last night that she's got the soul of a prim French provincial maid inside the shape of a waterfront whore. The only signals I received from her consisted of "Hands off".'

'Wise girl! But what if the intruder climbed down to her balcony from the roof above her room?'

'That would mean he was one of the inmates of this place, because, as you've seen, the gate in the *zaguán* has an automatic lock and only the clients have keys. Since there's a wrought-iron *reja* across the window of Paulette's room that overlooks the patio, unless she opened her door he would have to have gone over the roof. I'll inspect it in daylight, while you can have a girlie tête-à-tête with her and get all the details. I'm going back to bed.'

'Jimmy!' Elena exclaimed. 'Where has he got to? Did you see him come out into the corridor?'

'No, I didn't. Presumably he's out to the wide.'

'Go and see,' ordered Elena.

'I haven't seen him since shortly after we left the discothèque.'

'That ghastly noisy place!' she moaned. 'The things I put up with for the service.'

'Come on! You know the Chief's relying on us for information about the background activities of these missing kids. Anyway the disco was great. Better than most of the ones in Madrid.'

'And you should know.' Elena suddenly remembered something. 'Jimmy said he was going to see some pals in La Nogalera and left us in the Calle San Miguel. You really had better go and see if he got back. Maybe he's in some sort of trouble.'

'I think you've got a soft spot for the wild Irish boy. Watch it, now.'

'Get off with you and see if Jimmy's in.' She pushed him out and slammed the door, bolting it firmly behind him.

Ángel found the same uniformed man knocking loudly on Jimmy's door. 'Have you seen the occupant of this room, sir?'

'He's a red-haired Irishman. I last saw him in a very drunken state at about three forty-five this morning in the Calle San Miguel, where he left us to go and look for some friends in La Nogalera.'

'He doesn't seem to hear. Let's see if we can't get this old door open.'

The policeman fiddled with the antiquated latch, then lifted the door bodily up on its hinges until it swung open. He switched on the light and they both gazed at the extreme disorder in the room. Various items of clothing were scattered on the unmade bed and on the floor, but of the red-haired Irish lad there was no sign. On the table was the rectangle of silver foil burnt brown at the centre. The policeman picked it up and sniffed at it gingerly.

'A drug-addict is he, sir?'

Ángel shrugged and bent down to look under the bed. There was nothing and no one, apart from three cockroaches transfixed by the sudden flood of light. Jimmy hadn't come home.

Luis Bernal was dreaming that he was chasing a psychopath, who was armed with a machete, up the steps of the Cuesta del Tago; as his own corpulent frame stumbled out of breath on the steep steps, the tall sallow-faced killer leered at him menacingly from the railings on the bend above. Luis awoke suddenly in a bath of perspiration and found Consuelo's left arm lying across his throat. That constriction must have been the cause of his nightmare, he concluded. Lifting her arm gently, he tried to slip from under the sheet without disturbing her. He checked his watch and saw that it was 7.45 a.m. He tiptoed to the balcony to see if the police driver had come for him. He wanted to get to Málaga by nine, when he expected Peláez to have completed the second autopsy on Antonio García, Palencia's plain-clothes man.

As he wet-shaved as quietly as possible he heard Consuelo stir.

'You're not off again so early, Luchi?'

'I have to go, love. There's a lot to do.'

'I can see we won't get a proper holiday before this case is over. How long do you think it will take?'

'There's no way of telling. In fact there are at least two cases: the national problem of the ETA *Militar* laying bombs in the resorts; and the curious local case of the five missing foreign youths. The terrorists appear to be changing tack, to judge by the very small device they exploded at Benalmádena last night. It could be that by ordering patrols and cordons on the beaches we've made it too difficult for them to use the same tactics as they've used elsewhere, so they're starting to place smaller charges in any available loose soil where they can hide it unobserved.'

'But that puts everyone in very great danger, Luis,' she said, sitting on the edge of the bed to comb her hair.

'It's certainly going to make the patrolling more difficult, because we'll have to try to cover all the entrances to hotels and apartments as well as the public gardens. Then there's the problem of the five missing foreigners. We've got nowhere with them – no leads at all.'

'Are you sure the disappearances are all related, Luis?'

'We can't be sure, but there's too much coincidence for them not to be.' He paused and looked at her as he started to put on his shirt and tie. 'You know that I feel the presence of a murderer there in Torremolinos? Last night I even dreamt I could see him. Do you think that's possible? To dream of someone you don't know for sure really exists?'

She nodded slowly. 'I suppose it's possible. After all, you might have seen him without realising it and something registered in your deep unconscious.'

'But if he really exists, this psychopathic serial murderer, he's likely to give every sign of complete outward normality, while watching in the shadows for new prey. I've no facts to go on, but it's a strong gut feeling.'

'I know you've had those feelings before, Luis, in other cases. Let's think about how he could carry out such deeds in such a busy resort. Do you think he lures these youths by some pretext to a secluded spot and there murders them?'

'If so, how does he dispose of the bodies, not to mention their clothing and luggage?'

'It would have to be a very remote place, up in the hills.'

'In which case he would need to use a vehicle, and since yesterday he'd have to pass through the Civil Guard checkpoints.'

'Or it could be a building in the middle of the town to which only he has access,' mused Consuelo.

'As usual your logical banker's mind makes me see the problem more clearly, love. Now, in such a built-up place as Torremolinos there are hardly any natural spots left where the bodies could be left without almost immediate discovery by some member of the public. Even the hills in the immediate vicinity are frequently traversed by thousands of holidaymakers. Or supposing the murderer disposed of the bodies at sea, he would find it difficult to take a boat – out of La Carihuela, say – without someone noticing something was wrong. In any case, by now we should have expected the first bodies to be washed up along the coast.'

'What if he keeps them in one of the buildings in the town? Since the resort must be almost one-hundred-per-cent full in August, it would be comparatively easy to find out if any dwelling or garage were unused, because the nearest neighbours would notice.'

'You're quite right. I'll tell Lista and Miranda, who are on the house-to-house enquiries, to ask about disused buildings. There are thousands of apartments of course, but the tenants ought to notice any bad smells – in this heat a corpse would begin to putrefy quickly.'

Consuelo shuddered.

'And they'll also notice if the flat next to them is empty, Luis, because that would be very unusual with the rents at the high-season peak. You can certainly rely on people's inquisitiveness.'

'We'll look into that.' Luis looked out of the window. 'The driver's here.'

'Shan't I make you some breakfast?'

'I'll have some in Torremolinos when we pick up Inspector Palencia. Now, have a pleasant time with your sister-in-law, but keep well away from the beaches and the public gardens, all of you.'

'That doesn't leave us with much to do. I'll suggest we take the children into Marbella to do some shopping and have lunch there.'

'A good idea, but don't sit in a restaurant window overlooking the promenade, promise?'

After the night's alarms, Inspectora Elena Fernández slept on until the growing cheery chatter of the holidaymakers on their way down to the beach woke her up at 10.45. She felt guilty at oversleeping, so rose at once to inspect herself for insect-bites in the cracked mirror above the handbasin. As she washed and then began to make up her face, she could hear

112

some of the foreigners protesting loudly in English beneath her window.

'They won't let us on to the beach! Have you ever heard of such a thing? The policeman won't say why.'

'We'll move on to somewhere else. This place is impossible.'

'It's the same all down the coast. Haven't you seen the English papers? It's the Basque terrorists planting bombs on the beaches!'

'But there hasn't been an explosion here, has there?'

'Not yet. Come on, let's go and have a hair of the dog in the Britannia.'

So the Madrid authorities hadn't been able to keep the news out of the foreign press, thought Elena. But, then, her chief had known it would be impossible to suppress such a big story, which would have gone winging round the world by now. She turned on her small transistor radio to catch the eleven o'clock bulletin on Radio Nacional.

When she was dressed, she leant over the balcony to see if she could find out what was happening far below on the beaches. Near the two English pubs, she caught sight of what seemed to be a general store, and decided she must go there straight after breakfast and buy some insecticide. Suddenly she saw, coming up the hill against the direction taken by the mass of gaily dressed tourists, a tall, lithe, dark-haired man with a swarthy complexion and staring eyes that seemed to look up at her window.

Elena shuddered involuntarily and drew back sharply as he turned his hungry menacing gaze straight at her. Could he be the eerie cat-lover she had glimpsed on the rooftop last night? She turned to the door and almost ran out to find Ángel Gallardo.

Superintendent Luis Bernal and Inspector Jorge Palencia, having lingered rather longer than they had intended over their hot croissants and coffee in a café in the Plaza de Andalucía, did not reach the military hospital until 9.20 a.m. They found Doctor Peláez in the laboratory with

113

his thick-rimmed glasses pushed up on to the front of his head in the manner of a pilot's goggles, while his pig-like myopic eyes were glued to the binocular microscope.

'Hah! We'll have an enlarged shot of that,' he was commenting to the local pathologist and a technician. 'You see? The transverse process of the first cervical vertebra is fractured, and the vertebral artery is torn.' He stood back for the local man to take a look. 'As you can imagine, blood tracks along the vessel into the base of the skull, causing death within a few moments.'

'I've never seen such a phenomenon, Doctor,' murmured the local pathologist in admiring tones.

'It's extremely rare of course, and until ten years ago it was thought that there was always a small aneurysm on the cerebral circulation, although no one ever could locate it. It's all described in Cameron and Mant, 1972.'

Still standing in the doorway, Bernal gave a polite cough to indicate his presence, which made Peláez look up.

'Oh, you've got here, then, Luis. I really must admit that you never call me out in vain. This is only the third such case I've seen.'

Bernal introduced Palencia, and then asked: 'What was the cause of the young policeman's death, Peláez?'

'Come with us, both of you, if you can stomach looking at a very tidily dissected cadaver.' He turned to the Málaga pathologist: 'I must congratulate you on your skill, Doctor. He's a wonderfully neat cutter, Luis.'

Impatient now at the technical gobbledygook and the customary, slightly false, mutual backslapping of the professionals, Bernal said: 'We're up to it. Lead the way.'

The four of them entered the chill of the ancient white-tiled mortuary where an old attendant turned down the sheet from the head of the pathetically young Antonio García, whose skull had been sawn asunder by the famous pathologist. Bernal felt the local inspector stumble at his side, and he caught hold of the white-faced officer's arm.

'Bear up, Palencia,' he muttered. 'It'll soon be over.'

114

'Now, gentlemen,' boomed Peláez almost histrionically, 'I want you to observe the right side of the neck under the lobe of the ear. See anything?'

Bernal bent close to look, his stomach churned by the heavy mixture of the smells of incipient putrefaction and formalin. 'No, there's no mark.'

The famous pathologist gently pulled down the fold of what had once been healthy lean skin that followed the curve of the underpart of the ear into the curly black hair of the scalp. 'Now what do you see?'

'A small abrasion, the size of a *perra chica*.'

'That's exactly right, Luis. It's almost exactly the diameter of an old five-céntimo piece.'

'There's a tiny irregular cut in it on one side.'

'Well done. We've had an enlarged photo made for you. Now, let's go back to your office, Doctor. You can clear up here now,' he said to the gloomy-faced ancient who seemed to be the sole guardian of that necrophagous place.

When they were gathered in the somewhat pleasanter surroundings of the military pathologist's office, that official asked: 'Shall I send for some coffee, señores?'

'A good idea,' said Peláez, looking at the white-faced detectives. 'Tell them to send some Carlos Tercero to lace it for these two.'

Bernal pulled out his packet of Káiser and offered them to the others before lighting up.

'Now, tell us about the cause of death in simple language, Peláez.'

'You know I never talk in layman's terms. The cause of death was traumatic subarachnoid haemorrhage due to cervical spine injury.'

Bernal had seen enough forensic reports in his long service to read the signs accurately. 'So it was homicide.'

'Almost certainly, since it's hard to account for its having occurred accidentally on a soft sandy beach. It's a very rare occurrence: the blow could have been professionally delivered, though sometimes it happens more arbitrarily, as in drunken brawls.'

'But exactly how did it happen?' asked Palencia quietly. 'The spine wasn't injured, was it?'

'It was a blow to the side of the neck below the ear – an area not dissected in routine autopsies. In any case the very small external mark is frequently missed because it is concealed by the normal skin-folds there.'

'How is the blow usually delivered?' queried Bernal.

'With the fist, the edge of the hand, or the shod foot.'

'Was he kicked when he was already on the ground?' asked Palencia with sudden anger.

'I don't think so. That tiny irregular indentation in the abrasion was probably made by a ring worn on the little finger of the left hand of the assailant.'

'So we're looking for a professional,' said Bernal. He thought it out for a few moments as Peláez bit the end off a half Corona and lit it with a match. 'The attacker was tall,' Bernal speculated, 'taller than the victim at any rate, and left-handed, wearing a signet-ring on his left little finger. He came upon García unawares from behind and slightly to the right, then delivered a chopping blow with the outer edge of his left hand to the victim's neck below the right ear.'

'That's it. That's how I should reconstruct it,' said Peláez approvingly. 'Once the vessel there is ruptured, which may be with or without fracture of the transverse process of the first vertebra, the brain haemorrhage is almost instantaneous.' He turned to Palencia. 'Your man would hardly have felt a thing after the initial and fatal blow.'

'Who the hell trains people to kill like that?' asked Palencia angrily.

'We do; the State does,' said Bernal quietly. 'Anyone who undergoes commando or special service unarmed-combat training. There must be a number of former servicemen trained in these techniques among the *etarras*.'

'I asked for a special close-up to be taken of the ring-mark for you, Luis,' said Peláez. 'You'll be able to match it to the actual ring, which must have a stone set in the middle of it – probably a diamond chip. Now you've only got to find its owner.'

The phone rang, and the local pathologist picked up the receiver. 'It's the chief of the Guardia Civil,' he whispered to Palencia. 'He wants to talk to you.'

'We'll wait for you outside,' said Bernal.

'No, please don't go.' Palencia listened earnestly to the caller, then put his hand over the mouthpiece. 'The Civil Guard surgeon can't discover the pathological reason for the death of their man found on the golf-course at the Parador last night. He's asking whether I know the cause of death of my plain-clothes man.'

'Tell him,' suggested Bernal, 'he would be wise to seek the expert services of Doctor Peláez, who just happens to be in tip-top professional form here in Málaga.'

Peláez puffed contentedly on his cigar and winked at Bernal. 'Troubles always come in threes, Luis.'

Elena Fernández banged on Ángel's door, but got no answer. She went down the outside stairs into the patio, and from there ventured up the other staircase towards the French girl's room. Ángel's curtains were tightly drawn, though the two side-windows were open wide. She took the opportunity of looking at the roof-terrace and the entrance to Paulette's room. The girl, Elena knew, was with the proprietor's wife on the ground floor. She tried the door-handle but found it locked. Catching hold of the iron *reja* that protected the window, Elena hauled herself up sufficiently to see on to the flat roof. There, on the edge of the whitewashed frieze, she could make out scuff-marks – probably made by rubber soles, she thought. So the intruder had climbed up here, then crossed the roof and gone over the outer wall to enter Paulette's room by the street balcony, which being more than twelve metres above the lane was unprotected by a grille.

Elena scrambled down rather guiltily as a curly-headed Moor put his head over the staircase below her.

'Psst! You want some grass? It's real good stuff.'

Elena went down towards him quickly and replied coolly: 'No, thank you. Did you happen to see the intruder who

117

attacked the French girl early this morning when it was still dark? He probably got away over that far wall and down into the garden of that house where the boy practises the trumpet all day.'

'Me? I see nothing. I praying with my Muslim friends in number five.' His comical face took on a pseudo-saintly expression. 'We smoke and pray all night. He your friend?' He pointed at Ángel's window.

'I met him last night for the first time.'

'He nice chap. He smoke grass I sell him.'

'Really? I'm not at all surprised to hear it,' she said loudly under Ángel's open window, the pane of which she now rapped sharply.

'No good calling,' said the Moroccan. 'He not there.'

'Not there?'

'No, I see him go early.'

With a very worried expression, Elena said goodbye and hurried through the *zaguán* into the lane.

As they were being driven back from Málaga to Torremolinos, Bernal suggested to Palencia that they stop off at the Parador de Golf.

'Since the provincial chief of the Guardia Civil has asked for your co-operation over the death of his agent, Palencia, perhaps he won't mind our taking a look at the scene of the crime.'

Soon after the turn off the N340 to Rompedizo airport, the police driver braked and turned left along a narrow, twisting, potholed road that ran past the army camp and then crossed the railway line before changing into an attractive driveway lined with flower-beds stocked with pink, red and white oleanders, ivy-leaved pelargoniums and bright orange calendulas. The car pulled up before the squat modern façade of the State Parador, where they could see two Civil Guard jeeps parked.

The interior of the hotel was a cool dark contrast to the sticky heat of the littoral, where it seemed the dreaded *terral* wind was beginning to lift the dust.

'I'll order us apéritifs at the bar while you go and find the officer in charge, Palencia. What will you have?'

'Only a *bíter Kas* without alcohol, please, Comisario; I'd better keep a clear head.'

Bernal asked the well-spoken young barmaid for the red herbal drink, as well as a *doble* of draught beer for himself. Noticing her severe black dress and white frilly apron, he remembered how the young ladies who worked in the State *albergues de camino* and *paradores* in Franco's time were drawn mainly from the daughters of well-off families who served out their compulsory stint of *Servicio Social* in these respectable establishments. He noticed that there was still a certain *hauteur* about the service, as though the guests were being done something of a favour.

Bernal took the drinks to a table in the window that overlooked the swimming-pool and the last green of the golf-course beyond. The sea formed a shimmering grey edge to the peaceful scene, the bending light giving the impression that the horizon was higher than where he sat and that the breakers would engulf the hotel at any moment.

He plumped himself into an enormous brown leather-covered armchair and closed his eyes. Was all this becoming too much for him? he wondered. Shouldn't he request early transfer to the A Reserve List and take things more easily? But there was still so much to be done: it would surely take yet another change of government before a minister would be appointed with sufficient determination to undertake a root-and-branch reform of the various police forces and bestow a proper professionalism on them. He had hoped to be in the service long enough to witness the old Dictatorship links with the Army broken, the deep-rooted political interference from extremist groups ended and, above all, the corrupt contacts with common criminals eradicated.

He had always tried to run his Homicide Group in the Brigada Criminal on lines as professional as those in any other European country, and he hoped his protégé, Zurdo, recently promoted to head a group of his own, would continue the tradition. But the old battles between the *profesionalistas* and the *militaristas* had not died with the return of democracy. Perhaps he should go on as long as he could, so as not to leave room for any more vultures to gain positions of power in the Judicial Police.

Inspector Palencia now returned and picked up his drink. '*Salud*, Comisario.'

Bernal reciprocated the toast. 'What have they found?'

'Nothing of interest. The Civil Guard captain is coming in to talk to you. The Parador groundsman is still sounding off about the bumps left in his green around the marker-flag.'

'What bumps?'

'The intruders who appear to have killed the guard in the same way as they killed my man at Torremolinos cut up the turf round the eighteenth hole and left bumps in it.'

Bernal became extremely alarmed. 'Have they sent for a metal-detector?'

'No, I don't think so. They've assumed the intruders were disturbed by the guard before being able to plant anything.'

'Just like your man in Torremolinos did, but this business sounds much more ominous. The cordon they set up last night failed to catch the intruders as they escaped, didn't it? So perhaps they're still here. Come on! We'd better run.'

Despite his awkwardly squat, pot-bellied figure which was never subjected to unnecessary exercise, Bernal was capable, as his colleagues had often found to their cost, of putting on a considerable burst of speed. Now running past the guests lounging on the sparse grass round the rectangular swimming-pool, he shouted: 'Get indoors, all of you! Take cover, there's a bomb alert!'

Palencia ran after him as best he could, and at the gate dividing the Parador gardens from the golf-course they bumped into the Civil Guard captain.

'Have you cleared everyone from that green?' asked Bernal, waving his *comisario*'s badge at him.

'No, there doesn't seem to be any danger now.'

'It'll be a bomb, man! Get them away from there!'

120

At that moment two golfers on the eighteenth tee shouted 'Fore!' at the group of men standing on the edge of the fairway by the last green, and the first of them lofted a magnificent straight high shot.

'Keep your fingers crossed!' yelled the player. 'I'm going to hole in one.'

As they both watched with bated breath, the ball came sweeping down towards the centre of the eighteenth green, but then there was a sudden deep roar, followed by an ear-splitting explosion. Bernal, closely followed by Palencia, had almost reached the edge of the green when it cracked apart like a sheet of ice being pierced by an underwater monster surfacing, and tons of earth, gravel and stones were raised in a dark mass that began to scatter and fall over a considerable area.

Palencia, knocked flat by the blast, picked himself up and looked about him for the Comisario, of whom there was no trace. Good God, had he been caught by the bomb itself? Not noticing his own torn and mud-encrusted clothing, Palencia turned and met the Civil Guard captain, whose lip was bleeding. 'Where's Comisario Bernal?'

They searched the devastated green and saw two figures lying immobile by the edge of the fairway. Running towards them, the captain shouted: 'Those are my men. Radio for an ambulance.'

Still dazed, Palencia circled the great piles of broken turf, upchurned sand and scattered stones without seeing any human remains, then turned down the fairway where the captain was offering first aid to his wounded men. The local inspector was deeply worried. Surely Bernal hadn't got near enough to the hole to have been blown into pieces? Palencia wandered away from the large crater into the rough towards the sea's edge, where the cicadas had recommenced their high-pitched, almost deafening *cri-cri*, and the black scorpions surreptitiously scurried.

From there Palencia could see that the hotel guests had managed to beat a rapid retreat from the poolside to take refuge inside the Parador, which looked undamaged. From the beach a small group of holidaymakers and two fishermen carrying oars were making their way quickly to the scene of destruction.

Not far from where Palencia was searching, one of the fishermen shouted to his fellow: 'Come on! There's a body down there in that bunker.'

Palencia thought his heartbeat had ceased, then it began to race madly. He set off at a run for the spot where the fisherman had pointed.

Forgetting her hunger and thirst, Inspectora Elena Fernández walked quickly down the winding path of the Cuesta del Tago and took the left turn to the wider side-road where the garage of the Hotel Paraíso was cut out of the cliff. She passed a large boarded-up building and entered the rear entrance of the hotel, where a lift took guests from the carpark to the upper lobby. She pressed the button for the mezzanine floor, where most of the public rooms were situated, and there she strode into Navarro's office.

'Paco,' she gasped. 'Ángel's disappeared.'

Navarro grinned. 'He hasn't, you know; he's trying to locate the Chief urgently.'

She groaned and slumped into a chair. 'Can I ask for some coffee to be sent up?'

'Go ahead. We've had some. Ángel came in over an hour ago to say that your Irish friend Jimmy – he consulted a file-card – 'actually his full name is James Aloysius Collins, from Cork – can't be found and may be the latest missing youth. Ángel searched his room this morning and found his passport and traveller's cheques intact, so he can't have moved out under his own steam. We've had his passport photograph copied and we've sent it to all Palencia's men and to Lista and Miranda. Before putting out a general call, we wanted to get the Chief's say-so.'

Elena looked at her watch: it was well past noon. 'Why on earth didn't Ángel wake me?'

'He said he thought you needed some beauty sleep after your *juerga* in the clubs and discos last night.' The phone rang peremptorily, and Navarro dived for it. 'Inspector Palencia? Yes. Good God! Where? Is it serious? Where's he being taken?' He listened to the staccato reply and turned white-faced towards Elena. 'Yes. I'll send somebody at once.'

'What's happened?' demanded Elena anxiously.

'It's the Chief. There's been an explosion at the Parador. He's being taken first to the first-aid post at the airport nearby.'

Hoping no one had seen him entering the *comisaría* in the Plaza de Andalucía, Ángel Gallardo handed the Irishman's photograph to Palencia's sergeant for distribution to all units, and slipped out into the side-alley that led to the main street and the Plaza de la Costa del Sol. There he saw two ambulances and a fire-engine racing past in the direction of Málaga, and wondered what was up. He decided to retrace his steps of the early hours from the fashionable discothèque to the Calle de San Miguel to the point where Jimmy had left them.

When he reached that point, Ángel turned into La Nogalera, where the terraces were filling up with people taking pre-prandial drinks – far more people than on other days, he noticed, presumably because the beaches were temporarily cordoned off. He ran his eye along the raised beds of trees and lawns in the centre of the busy square, where young foreigners sunbathed and chatted. He did not miss the occasional sly passing of drugs among that international throng and he guessed that that was what Jimmy had been seeking there during the early hours. But where had he gone after that? Shiny new arcades and alleyways led off in every direction: it was futile trying to guess which way Jimmy had gone, or who had lured him away. As he stopped to take in the animated scene, an idea slowly formed in his mind. That was it! A stake-out. He would put the idea to the Chief as soon as he managed to locate him. He ought to get Elena up and talk the plan over with her.

He cut through the modern arcade, past the cafés, restaurants, bars and discothèques, until he reached the Calle de Casablanca. From there he took a short-cut through the

Pasaje de San Miguel to the Windmill restaurant and the steps leading down to the Bajondillo. From outside the Casa España he saw the maid shaking the mattress on the balcony of Jimmy's room. That struck him as very odd, and he hastened across the semi-conscious bulk of Rémy and hurried up the stairs. He found the door of the Irishman's room wide open and the maid busily washing down the floor.

'Where's Jimmy?'

'He checked out this morning.'

'Did he come himself to get his things?'

'No, that's the strange thing. A friend of his collected them for him.'

'Did you see the person who took them?'

'Only for a moment when he was leaving with the luggage. That was when the boss' – she made a grimace – 'told me to clean the room.'

Stopping only to bang loudly on Elena's door, Ángel started back down the stairs two at a time.

'She's gone out, that girlfriend of yours,' the maid shouted after him. 'About an hour ago.'

'Did she say where she was going?'

'She doesn't as much as say "How d'ye do" to the likes of me,' she sniffed.

The stout proprietor was working on his accounts in the front parlour, while his wife was pouring a coffee in the back room for the still tearful Paulette, who looked soulfully out at Ángel and then put her head on her arms and began to sob loudly once more.

'She's cried all night long,' said the lodging-keeper. 'We're both worn out.'

'Did Jimmy the Irishman come himself to get his belongings this morning or inform you he was leaving?'

'No, but he telephoned.'

'What time was that?'

'Around ten forty-five. He said he was at the airport trying to change his ticket to fly back to Dublin at once, because his father had been taken seriously ill. He said he was sending a friend to collect the things from his room.'

124

'And how were you to recognise this friend?'

'He would show me Jimmy's international student-card with his photo on it, which he did, soon after the call. Why all the questions?'

Ángel was still anxious not to blow his cover. 'It's just that we were very worried about Jimmy last night; he was high and left us on the way back.'

'Hey, you don't think it was him who attacked Paulette and then decided to skip?'

'Is that what she says?'

'No, she says it was a dark-haired man. She's still very scared. She won't tell us what the intruder did to her.' The proprietor nudged Ángel's elbow in a prurient gesture.

'I shouldn't have thought he had time to do anything, the way she started yelling.'

'I'm not so sure. My wife thinks he did something – something really nasty – to the girl. She didn't half scream, eh?' He licked his lips in a lascivious manner. 'She's too frightened even to look out of the window today.'

'So what did this friend of Jimmy's look like? Was he foreign, too? Irish?'

'No, I'm sure he was a native speaker of Spanish, though he didn't say much. He had a regional accent – from round here, I'd say. I think I've seen him about once or twice in the past couple of months.'

'You mean he's local, then? Perhaps working in a travel agency?'

'That could be, though he said he was the Irishman's friend. Funny, that. He was a strange fellow: very tall with a dark complexion. Odd look in his eyes. Why do you want to know all this?'

'I'm really worried that Jimmy has fallen into bad company – drug-pushers and so on.'

'He'll be OK; he's probably on the plane by now.'

Ángel went across the road to the Red Lion and found the public phone free. 'Paco? All of Collins's stuff has been removed from the *pensión* by someone posing as his friend. Will you ring Rompedizo and find out if the Irishman booked

125

a flight to Dublin, or possibly to London or Manchester, for today?'

'Will do. Listen, Ángel, I've got very bad news for you. There's been an explosion at the Parador de Golf. It's the Chief – he was almost on top of the bomb. You'd better come straight in: Elena's already here.'

'I'm on my way.'

Inspector Palencia rushed to the fisherman's side and looked down into the sandy bunker that had once defended the eighteenth hole of the course. There Superintendent Bernal lay with his eyes closed and his body half-covered by greyish dust; blood ran down from his left temple on to his shirt-front. The Inspector climbed gingerly down the half-collapsed side of the ditch and took hold of the Superintendent's left wrist. Thank God, there was still a sluggish pulse. Palencia took the white handkerchief from Bernal's breast-pocket, unfolded it to get the clean side out, and rolled it to staunch the wound.

Bernal began to stir slightly and tried to open his eyes, though the left one was covered in blood. 'Palencia?' he murmured. 'Tell them to seal off the grounds of the Parador and set up road-blocks straight away.'

As Palencia hesitated, Bernal tried to sit up and took hold of the rolled handkerchief the Inspector was pressing hard on the wound. 'Go on, man. I'll be all right. Get the Captain to take action and search the hotel. They'll still be here on the premises. If he acts quickly, he'll catch them.'

Now convinced that Bernal was not about to expire, the Inspector told the fisherman: 'Make sure he keeps the wad pressed to the wound and look after him while I get help.'

What had been the eighteenth green now looked like a battlefield, and in the centre of it Palencia came across the Civil Guard captain, half-stunned, looking down at his injured men.

'Is your radio transceiver working, Captain? The Comisario wants you to set up road-blocks immediately. I suggest one to the south on the Torremolinos road, another on the Málaga

126

road, and a third between here and the airport. The Superintendent also wants an immediate cordon thrown round the grounds of the Parador. He thinks the bombers are still in the vicinity.'

The Captain made an effort to pull himself together and called in to the Civil Guard central control to give the orders. 'Shall I call for ambulances?'

'Ask them to check whether they're on their way. I expect the hotel staff will have got on to the emergency services. We must make sure nobody leaves the building.'

As they entered the hotel lobby, the sound of sirens could be heard. The local inspector gave instructions to the hotel manager and then telephoned the chief of police in Málaga to request reinforcements.

When the first of the ambulancemen entered, Palencia directed them to the golf-course. 'There's a *comisario* from Madrid lying injured in a bunker near the green. Follow me.'

On reaching the spot, they found Bernal sitting on the edge of the ditch, smoking a Káiser. A grubby scarf had been tied piratically round his head to hold the cotton wadding in place.

'I'm all right now, Palencia. Get them to take the seriously wounded first.'

'But you're probably going to need stitches put in that wound, Chief. You'd better go in the ambulance to the military hospital in Málaga.'

'That place? Not on your life. Where's the nearest first-aid post?'

'At the airport.'

'Very well. There's sure to be a doctor. Our police driver will run me there in the car. I'm only one of the walking wounded.' He waved the ambulancemen towards the men lying near the fairway. 'Palencia, have you got a set of those mugshots of the *etarra* suspects?'

'There's a set in the car.'

'Good, let's go and show them to the hotel staff. Has the cordon been set up?'

'They're doing it now.'

'It's probably too late, but help me into the hotel, will you?'

In the manager's office, Bernal accepted a cup of heavily sweetened tea, then insisted on ringing Navarro.

'It's me, Paco.'

'Thank God you're safe, Chief. Are you injured? Elena is on her way to you.'

'There's no need. And it's only a small cut on the forehead. Has Varga arrived with the technical team?'

'We've had a message to say they should be here this afternoon. He had problems in Madrid in assembling them.'

'Good, we're going to need his help. I want that cigarette-butt I collected on the beach at Torremolinos analysed, especially to see if they can do a "blood-print", assuming the smoker was a secreter. We know the blood groups of some of these *etarras* who were arrested on previous occasions.'

Bernal now asked the harassed manager if he recognised any of the people in the set of police photographs. He shook his head doubtfully, then said: 'You'd better ask the desk-clerk. He sees the guests much more than I do.'

That well-dressed young man was sent for, and was asked to look through the small pile of mugshots. He turned them over slowly until he got to the last one, then he went back to the fourth of them. 'This woman – she could be the woman in room twenty-three, though she looks different now. It's the hairstyle, I think, that's changed.'

Bernal took the card and looked at the details printed on the back. 'Was there a man with her?'

'Yes, a bearded fellow who always wears sunglasses, even at night.'

'And he's not among these?'

The man went back through the remaining photos and then returned to the third one. 'He could just be this one, but the man in this photo is much younger and clean-shaven.'

Bernal took the card and turned to Palencia: 'Get up to room twenty-three and take some armed guards with you.'

'But they aren't there now, sir,' said the desk-clerk. 'They went off in their car just after the explosion.'

'Damn!' exclaimed Bernal. 'Did they check out?'

'No, sir. It looked as though they were just going out.'

'Were they carrying any luggage?'

'I didn't see any, sir, but I was busy dialling 091 for the emergency services right then.'

'What make of car did they have?'

'A white Fiat, I think, but if you hold on for a moment I can get its *matrícula* from our computer. All the guests have to give us details of their vehicles.'

'Please do, as quickly as you can.'

The clerk went into the accounts office and tapped out the room number on the microcomputer. 'Here you are; I thought it a bit odd at the time. It's an old Málaga registration – not a hire car – while virtually all our guests have numbers from other provinces or from abroad.'

'Get the Captain to put this number out and the vehicle description to all Civil Guard traffic patrols, Palencia,' said Bernal urgently. 'Then get on to Vehicle Registration Records and see who the car belongs to.'

By the time Bernal had been driven to the airport, where a doctor had put three stitches in the deep wound across his left eyebrow and dressed it, at the patient's insistence, only with a piece of sticking plaster to hold the lint in place, the small white Fiat used by the supposed terrorists had been found hidden in a clump of eucalyptus trees near the railway line, just off the narrow road leading from the Parador to the N340.

'So they were too quick off the mark to get caught by the cordon,' commented Bernal to a disappointed Inspector Palencia, when he returned to the Parador. 'They ran along the railway line, I suppose.'

'We think they got to Campamento station nearby.'

'Have you ordered checks on all the stations between here and Málaga to the north and Fuengirola to the south?'

'Yes, Comisario, but it's probably too late. If they jumped on to a southbound train, they could have got off at Torremolinos station and quickly mingled with the crowds in La Nogalera.'

'It's worth ringing RENFE and asking them about the actual departure times of the trains from Campamento during the past hour. That way we could find out whether they went on the up line or the down.'

'I have, and they're going to phone me back here.'

'At least all this confirms my guess that they must have detonated the bomb by remote control, otherwise they wouldn't have stayed until the actual explosion.'

'I'm still puzzled by why you were so sure a bomb would go off when none of the Civil Guards expected it. Your shouts of warning saved a lot of lives, Chief.'

'There are still five casualties, Palencia, two of them serious. But what alerted me was what you said about the groundsman being upset at the bumps in his turf. Now, last night the Civil Guard officer assumed that his man disturbed the intruders just as they were beginning to lift the turf near the hole on the eighteenth green. But if there were raised lumps under the cut turf it suggested that the bombers were finishing their work, rather than beginning it, when they were disturbed. After all, no bomb was found and they hardly had time to carry it off unobserved when the dead guard was found so quickly and the alarm raised.'

'But they could have run off with it along the beach,' objected Palencia.

'Then the cordon should have picked them up,' answered Bernal. 'No, I concluded that they had simply merged with the other guests in the Parador attracted by the disturbance. They could hardly have done that if they were lumbered with an infernal device. The only question is: what did they do with the spade? We must question the groundsman.'

'Is there anything else we should do?'

'Yes. As soon as Varga and his technical team arrive from Madrid, I want them to go over room twenty-three and the white Fiat in a detailed search. They are sure to have left fingerprints somewhere, especially in the hotel room.' Bernal lit a cigarette and sat back in the chair. 'At least we've done better than the other groups up till now, Palencia: we've got two names of bombers to transmit to Madrid.' A further thought struck him. 'What if the ETA commandos are using the Paradors all along the coast? Unlike hotel or apartment-owners, the directors don't expect their guests to stay for a fortnight or a month; these places are meant for visitors who are touring by road and who spend only a few days in each place.'

'Let's point that out to the Anti-Terrorist Command in Madrid, Comisario, and get all the coastal Paradors checked out.'

When Bernal returned to the Hotel Paraíso in Torremolinos he was greeted like a returning soldier by his colleagues.

'You ought to go back to Cabo Pino and lie down for the rest of the day, *jefe*,' urged Elena.

'There's too much to do. Is there any news from the controls at the railway stations?'

'Nothing so far, Chief,' said Navarro.

'Then, we've lost them for the moment. At least we know which pair to look for now.'

Miranda came in to report a breakthrough in the *pensión*-to-*pensión* enquiries. The Interpol photograph of the missing Italian youth, Salvatore Croce, had been recognised by a lodging-house keeper on the Paseo Marítimo. It was typical of Bernal, despite the remonstrations of all his colleagues, to insist on going to interview the witness in person.

'There's one serious matter before you go, Chief,' said Ángel. 'There seems to have been another disappearance – that of an Irishman called Jimmy Collins, who was with Elena and myself last night. Here's my initial report.'

As Bernal scanned through the document, Navarro said: 'At Ángel's request I contacted all the airlines at Rompedizo, and no one of that name changed or bought a ticket to leave Málaga today.'

'I've thought of a plan, Chief,' said Ángel excitedly. 'A stake-out tonight in La Nogalera, where Jimmy was last known to be. I could go to the disco with Elena and then in the early hours she could fake a row with me in the Calle San Miguel about drug-taking and then march off to the *pensión* in disgust. From there I could enter the small clump of trees in the square and join the usual group of drug-addicts and drunks, and pretend to be semi-conscious. You could have the whole square staked out with plain-clothes squads with help from the local inspector, and I could take one of the miniature Japanese transceivers to keep in touch. It could be the psychopath will fall for the bait.'

Bernal considered the plan gravely. 'It would have to be very carefully arranged, Ángel,' he said slowly, thinking over the possibilities, 'but it may be worth a try. The disappearances are becoming more frequent, just as we feared. I discussed the problem with Doctor Peláez, who thinks the increasing rhythm a dangerous development.' Bernal turned to Navarro. 'Is there nothing in from Central Records about any pattern of missing persons elsewhere?'

'Inspector Ibáñez rang through earlier. He says the main-frame computer hasn't come up with any noticeable pattern in any province. There have been nineteen cases of missing male adolescents during the past year, but they've been scattered throughout the national territory – mainly in the big cities. There's nothing to indicate a maniac at large until the disappearances here during the past month.'

'That's odd, isn't it? It's almost as though this criminal had come in from abroad. Has he tried the Interpol records?'

'They are investigating, Chief, because of the reports sent in to them from the worried parents of the missing foreign youths here.'

'We'll have to see if they come up with anything.' Bernal turned to Ángel. 'You really want to run the risk of being the bait in this kind of stake-out?'

'If you give me all the necessary back-up, *jefe*.'

'Naturally. Every angle must be covered. Work something out with Paco and Inspector Palencia, will you, while I go down and interview this lodging-house keeper.' Bernal asked Miranda to accompany him. 'Oh, before I forget, Paco. When Varga arrives, ask him to test that cigarette-butt I picked up on the beach, as well as doing a thorough forensic examination of the white Fiat and room twenty-three at the Parador. He may be able to match up some traces with the blood groups of the bombers.'

132

The *pensión* in the Paseo Marítimo consisted of a flat-roofed three-storey building near the Montaña Acuática where children in bathing-costumes were climbing excitedly to the top of the water-filled slide of the helter-skelter to sit on rubber cushions for the thrilling and twisting descent that would plunge them into a small pool at the base. The shops at street level, forming a continuous line of sunshades and beach accessories, proffered suntan lotions, candy-floss and ice-creams, foreign newspapers and magazines, and other aids to lounging on the sand. Small staircases between the shops led to the boarding accommodation.

Miranda led Bernal up one of these flights to a tiny entrance-hall where an old man was watching the 'Telediario' newscast. Bernal watched the screen for a moment to see if there was any reference in the headlines to the bombs laid in the coastal resorts. No doubt the Interior Ministry would attempt to get the events played down.

The old man looked at Bernal's torn clothing with curiosity and then at his official badge; he nodded at Miranda, who had questioned him earlier.

'Will you tell me when this Italian youth arrived here?' asked Bernal, showing him the police photograph.

'As I've already told the Inspector, he took the room on Friday the twenty-third of July; here's the registration-card which he signed. He paid for six nights in advance, saying he would leave on the twenty-ninth to catch his return flight to Milan. But he left after only four nights.'

'Did he tell you why when he went off with his luggage?'

'He didn't tell me anything and he didn't take his luggage. A man came to collect it for him on the morning of the twenty-seventh, because that's when I relet the room. The man brought Croce's passport with him and said that his friend's mother was dangerously ill and that he was at the airport on stand-by for the next available flight home.'

'But how could you have been certain that this stranger wasn't a thief who had stolen Croce's passport?'

'He showed me a note written by the lad, but it was in Italian, so I couldn't really understand it.'

'Did you compare the signature on the note with the one on the registration-card?'

'No, I didn't think of it,' admitted the man.

'This man who said he was Croce's friend, had you ever seen him before?'

'No, but he was a native speaker of Spanish, I'm sure.'

'Would you agree to try to make a Photofit picture of him up at our office?'

The man nodded. 'I'm sure I would recognise him again: he was tall and well built, with staring eyes.'

'Have you still got the note he brought?'

'I don't know what happened to it.' He looked at the untidy desk-top. 'Come to think of it, he probably took it with him.'

Bernal looked at Miranda. 'He's careful to leave no traces, isn't he?' He turned back to the landlord. 'Would you come with us now and piece together bits of photographs until you have a reasonable likeness of the man who took the luggage?'

'I'll just call my daughter to take over the desk.'

Bernal was finally persuaded to return to Cabo Pino after taking a light lunch in the hotel. 'You need a shower and a change of clothes, Chief,' said Navarro. 'Then you can take a good rest before tonight's special operation.'

'Very well, but I'll be back at nine p.m. to go over the details of the plan you come up with.'

Only when the police driver dropped him off outside the duplex apartment did Luis remember Consuelo had gone to Marbella for the day with her sister-in-law, and the children he had not yet seen, since they appeared to live in a world and on a time-scale quite different from his own.

At dusk the tall stranger stirred from his peculiar dwelling and started to fill two plastic carrier-bags with offal from the refrigerator. His wild-cats would soon be feeling hungry – this was the time when the sun had gone down and the

134

breeze changed direction: Feeding Time! They had been very angry with him the other night when he had got there so late because of stupid circumstances beyond his control, he remembered, twisting his facial muscles into a grim moue. Well, he had sorted that nonsense out, with a vengeance. With a vengeance – that's what all this was for: to wreak revenge on vicious creatures.

He looked out through a crack in the boarded-up window: now it was almost completely night – that velvety darkness filled with the residual heat of the sun, and the smells of the upper part of the town as the offshore breeze of evening reversed the airflow pattern of the day. He slipped outside with his stinking packages and at once felt the night caress him like a warm dark garment.

Luis Bernal was woken by a kiss planted on his cheek and he let himself relax deeper into the luxurious mattress.

'Luchi?' Consuelo whispered. 'What happened to your head? Did you fall down?'

He rolled over towards her. 'I'll tell you when we have our pre-dinner drinks. Did you have a good time in Marbella?'

She looked at the pile of dusty and torn clothes on the floor near the window and picked them up critically. 'Now, come on, tell me what happened. Were you in a road accident?'

'No, love, just a small explosion.'

By 10 p.m., with his strength restored, Bernal had gone over the detailed plan to stake out La Nogalera square from 2 a.m. onwards, when the bars would start to close for the night. Positions would be taken up from 1.30 by five squads of plain-clothes men led by Inspector Palencia, Miranda, Lista, Elena Fernández and Navarro. Bernal would be placed at a central control point in the upper windows of a travel agency that overlooked the entire square, from where he would be in constant radio contact with all the squads and with Ángel, who would provide the bait

135

in the grassy area in front of the bar-terraces.

First, Elena and Ángel would return to their *pensión* as though they had been out for the day, and then they would set off to have supper and afterwards take in some bars and clubs before going to the discothèque that Elena hated so much, swearing that her hearing had been permanently damaged by the excessive decibel level there the night before. Tonight she was taking the precaution of using an unobtrusive pair of small earplugs.

Navarro's vantage-point above a bar on the corner of the Calle de San Miguel and La Nogalera, not far from their office in the Hotel Paraíso, would enable him to be the first to give the other units warning of Ángel and Elena's return from the discothèque. There would then ensue the staged quarrel and Elena's departure in simulated high dudgeon. Once at the end of San Miguel she would return discreetly through the modern shopping-precinct to take up position with her plain-clothes men at the first-floor restaurant that overlooked La Nogalera on the eastern side.

The other three squads commanded the only other exits from the square, so that it was impossible for Ángel to leave or be lured from his central position without this being spotted at once by one or more of the five units, who had been instructed to follow at a discreet distance unless Ángel called for assistance on his transceiver.

After feeding his wild-cats on the rooftops of the Bajondillo, the tall stranger thought about his human supper preparations. He'd better make it a light meal tonight; too much protein produced an excessive, almost uncontrollable strength. He'd have to watch out.

Before vaulting back over the railings he looked up at the balcony of the Casa España; it was in darkness tonight. That girl with the inquisitive nose and her lover must have gone out early. The tall stranger with the unquiet disquieting glance set off with a springing step on the path that led down towards the sea. It was too early to venture up into the town.

*   *   *

136

Despite all Consuelo's pleadings earlier, Bernal could not be dissuaded from leading the stake-out operation. The police driver collected him at Cabo Pino at 10 p.m. and made slow progress through Fuengirola and beyond through the continuous ribbon of seaside towns. The main coast-road was brightly lit by flashing neon signs advertising *tablaos* of flamenco dancing, hamburger joints, flashy bars, garish discothèques, bingo halls and live-show nightclubs. The nocturnal air was thick with dust particles and exhaust fumes; although the *terral* had dropped, it had left the atmosphere unpleasantly stirred up. The humid heat of the day had barely subsided, and Superintendent Bernal perspired heavily under the collar of his new shirt.

He hoped he was doing the right thing in allowing this stake-out to go ahead. From long experience he knew that things could go badly wrong: there was always an unexpected factor that no one had foreseen. Still, Ángel Gallardo would be armed with a small revolver and would be carrying a miniature Japanese transceiver of the latest type with a microphone hidden under his shirt collar. He would also be very closely watched by the five plain-clothes units from the moment he set foot in La Nogalera. Bernal lit a Káiser and tried to relax in the back seat of the black SEAT 134.

At 12.40 a.m. the tall lithe stranger made his way back to the steps of the Cuesta del Tago and began to climb towards the Windmill restaurant. He stopped to look down at the foreshore, which was in darkness tonight. He had heard about the bombs on Cadena SER: none had gone off in Torremolinos, but a brief account was given of the explosion at the Parador de Golf. Perhaps the beaches would be open to the public again tomorrow.

As he continued his ascent, he glanced at the young people who went merrily by, ignoring his presence. One day they would find out how bitter life really was; they were living in a fool's paradise at that age, he thought. His lip curled into a cruel leer as he turned into the arcade past La Fuente restaurant in the new shopping-precinct. He slipped from the small square, where a tiny fountain tinkled, through the narrow passageway into the dark jasmine-scented patio beyond, a place which few tourists noticed. From here a two-metre-wide alley, which had once been a main thoroughfare in the old fishing village, ran behind the new restaurants, ice-cream parlours and art galleries almost all the way to La Nogalera square.

It was his favourite approach: from the lovely dark alley that belonged to him alone he could peer out unobserved at the colourfully lit and thickly populated square, for this was the secret path to his stalking-ground. Now he hesitated: something was different tonight; there was a subtle scent of danger. He looked round at the bright scene from his shadowy vantage-point. What could be wrong?

Superintendent Bernal felt as though he was the director of an enormous stage: below him was spread much of the nightlife of Torremolinos. Its devotees had perforce to cross and re-cross this focal point at some time during the after-midnight hours as they reeled from one club or discothèque to another, some stopping for a chat or a friendly tussle, others trying to pick up new partners, yet others seeking soft or hard drugs from the pushers. With his 30 × 70 night prismatics, Bernal could pick out every detail of the grassy area dominated by three large magnolia trees. Bernal checked that the five units were in their allotted places; it was absurd to think that any serious harm could befall his young inspector under such massive surveillance.

Now the scene was set: only Ángel and Elena had yet to make their first-act entrance.

The tall lithe stranger sat on an upturned orange-box watching the scene from the dark opening of the old alley. He suddenly thought it was like being *entre bastidores* – in the wings of a great theatre, whence you could see everything that occurred on the vast floodlit stage, and even beyond, in the auditorium illuminated by reflected light; but no one at all could see you. This idea gave him a feeling of immense power, yet tonight he sensed for the first time the presence of an opposing force, a hidden threat to his usual activities.

He glanced slowly round at the buildings that framed the irregularly shaped square. It must be his imagination playing tricks again; there was nothing wrong. Just then he caught sight of the inquisitive girl from the *pensión* down the hill engaged in a loud argument with her handsome young man, who was reeling as though drunk or drugged. That girl with the pointed nose: how he hated her! She had leant out of her window to try to see what he was doing on the rooftop opposite; she was trying to invade his secret world.

Now she was slapping the handsome young man across the face and next thing she stalked off down the Calle de San Miguel. The tall lithe stranger watched with a growing predatory stare as the handsome young man staggered into La Nogalera and slumped to the ground under the magnolia tree. Just like Keller, the German boy. The tall man smiled as he remembered. This one wasn't quite the type, perhaps. He saw the handsome young man draw himself up on to one elbow and sniff something from a tinfoil sheet. Ah, a smack-addict, for sure. Soon the young man would lose consciousness for a while, then he could move in.

The tall stranger looked round at the rapidly diminishing crowd in the square and at the two municipal policemen who strolled past on their beat. He had never found them a threat; on the contrary, they usually exchanged pleasantries with him and congratulated him on doing a good job for them. Still with an inexplicable feeling of ill-ease that made him look round once more at the darkened windows of the commercial offices in the square, he decided to emerge from his hiding-place on to the scene. Just then a vast number of white-suited foreigners jabbering excitedly burst into La Nogalera from the direction of the Plaza de la Costa del Sol.

Superintendent Bernal watched the staged quarrel between Ángel and Elena through his powerful binoculars and considered that they had played their parts very convincingly. He watched Elena march off down San Miguel and then admired

Ángel's solo piece as he staggered towards the magnolia tree and fell on to the grass. Bernal called up all five plain-clothes squads: 'Watch out for any solitary passer-by acting suspiciously.' He scanned all the approaches with the prismatics and thought he saw a movement in a dark entrance he had not noticed previously. As he was focusing the lenses on to that spot, there erupted into the square below him what seemed to be half the men of the United States Sixth Fleet, closely pursued by a group of harassed red-capped MPs.

Oh Lord! sighed Bernal. The stake-out would be ruined now. Where the hell had these sailors come from? He called Navarro over the radio. 'Come in, Paco. We might as well call it off: there must be over five hundred American sailors down there. Is there a ship in? Over.'

'I forgot to tell you, Chief. It's the USS *Nimitz*; she put into Málaga at 10.45 p.m. on a courtesy visit to give the men some shore leave. Palencia got a message from the Málaga police.'

'They're not doing us much of a courtesy, are they? They'll be crawling over every off-limits dive in the place until morning. We'd better abort the operation for tonight.'

Elena reached the end of the wide part of the Calle de San Miguel and then turned sharply into the Calle Casablanca. Glancing round to make sure she wasn't being followed, she cut through the arcade that led past the Restaurant La Fuente and from there entered the main pedestrian precinct that ran up to La Nogalera once more.

Halfway up the marble-paved precinct she passed two municipal policemen, when suddenly she saw a mass of white-uniformed men chasing and shouting in La Nogalera. What on earth was happening? She stiffened as she caught sight of a tall figure that seemed familiar, hurrying towards her from the square. Oh God, it was the cat-lover! An unexplained terror struck her at the sight of him. His strange burning glance bore into her as he passed, and she turned hastily to look into the window of an art gallery.

Looking sideways, she saw the municipal policemen greet the cat-lover and exchange remarks with him.

'No customers for you tonight, eh?' the older policeman said.

'No, the American fleet's in, and they've got their own MPs to look after them.'

The policemen laughed. 'Good night, then.'

The tall stranger disappeared down the alley that led to the small fountain, and Elena, with sudden decision, went back to the municipal policemen. She fished in her small evening bag for her warrant-card.

'I'm Inspectora Fernández of the DSE on special duties here. Who was that man you just spoke to?'

They looked doubtfully at her appearance and then at the DSE badge. The older man saluted and was quickly imitated by his younger companion.

'I don't know his real name, Inspectora, but he runs a relief agency for young people in trouble, especially drug-addicts. That's why he's always about late at night. The kids call him "The Angel of Torremolinos".'

'He's not Spanish, is he?'

'Argentinian or Uruguayan, we think. He used to be a missionary out there. He's been here for a couple of months, almost.'

'Do either of you know where he lives?'

'Not exactly, but it's somewhere down in the Bajondillo. We think he's quite genuine, Inspectora.'

'Thank you for your help. You see, we're on a special plain-clothes drugs-assignment operation here. That man might be useful to us for questioning.'

The two municipal policemen saluted again as she hurried away to take charge of her unit in La Nogalera.

'Strange-looking for an inspector from the Criminal Brigade in Madrid, isn't she?' commented the older policeman.

'In that low-cut orange dress with the tassels I thought she was on the game,' said the younger man. 'Wouldn't mind being run in by her.'

Elena Fernández soon found that her chief had called off the entire stake-out. The arrival of such a large naval contingent together with the presence of United States Navy police made the operation too difficult to bring off, Bernal had calculated. The psychopath, too, would have been discouraged, he guessed. The Superintendent picked up his night-glasses and took another look at the dark entrance where he had seen a movement before the distracting arrival of the American sailors. There was no one there now. He could make out only an upturned box, but he had sensed an evil presence there, almost as though it emitted fire and brimstone.

Were such presentiments entirely irrational? he wondered. Consuelo hadn't thought so, and she was the most logically minded person he knew. He resolved to inspect that entrance in daylight.

He asked himself how long they would have to go on with this business. There were no other clear leads to follow. The Photofit picture made up by the lodging-house keeper looked so improbably ill-favoured that he could not imagine anyone really looking like that, yet it had an indefinable feeling of evil about it. There was a psychopath on the loose, he was sure of that now. He had circulated the Photofit to all police units: perhaps someone would recognise him, unlikely as it seemed. He left his vantage-point and went back to the Hotel Paraíso to confer with his group.

At 7.55 a.m. on Thursday, 5 August, Consuelo Lozano stood shivering gently in her flimsy nightdress on the balcony of the duplex apartment at El Puerto de Cabo Pino, looking out for the arrival of the police car. She glanced back anxiously at Luis Bernal, half-turned towards her in deep slumber in the comfortable double-bed, with his brow nervously furrowed and his arms curiously entangled close to his chest in almost foetal manner. She bent to examine the plaster on his injured eyebrow for signs of seeping blood, and wondered whether it was time to persuade him to take early retirement. These sensational and perilous cases of a political nature seemed to sap what remained of his energies, and yesterday he had come so close to death. Oh, how could she bear it when he returned again and again to a job in which he was so often exposed to danger?

142

Consuelo crossed the bedroom silently and slipped on her terry-towelling bathrobe. For once there was a cool morning breeze; perhaps the wind was shifting round to the south-west from the strait. She hurried back to the window in order to forestall the police driver's merry tooting and to signal him to come in for a coffee and allow his chief a little more sleep.

A deep groan made her glance round; Luis was turning away from the light with his eyes screwed up. He gave a further twist to his enwrapped arms so that she marvelled that he didn't break a wrist or dislocate a shoulder; he would probably complain of cramp when he awoke.

Consuelo now saw the black SEAT emerge from the short road-tunnel and turn the corner on to the small palm-fringed promenade. When it halted, she began to make frantic gestures to the driver. Instead of blowing the horn as was his wont, he got out and looked up at her. She pointed at the door and indicated that he was to enter. As she turned to go down and make the coffee, Bernal suddenly sat up.

'Is the driver there?'

'How did you know? I was planning to give you an extra half-hour's rest. You didn't get in until well after three. How's your head?'

He touched the plaster gingerly and winced. 'Don't remind me. I've got a bit of a headache, that's all. Make some coffee for the driver, will you? I'll get shaved.'

She kissed him tenderly on the lips and made for the door. 'I hope this will be over soon, Luchi.'

'Nothing goes on for ever, love.'

In the temporary office at the Hotel Paraíso, Bernal found Inspector Navarro sorting through the reports that had come in that morning.

'Any news, Paco?'

'Morning, Chief. The white Fiat abandoned near the Parador de Golf has been traced. It was stolen in Málaga three days ago.'

143

'These *etarras* are certainly taking risks, aren't they? It could have been spotted at any time, since they can't have changed the number-plates.'

'No, they didn't; they're getting careless.'

'Or cheeky. Have you asked for a list of all vehicles stolen in the province since the Fiat was discovered yesterday? We should send a notice of the *matrículas* to all mobile units. The terrorists are bound to need some kind of transport.'

'I've asked Málaga to send the list out, with a telex copy to us.'

'Good. Did Palencia find out which train they are likely to have taken from Campamento station?'

'The next one straight after the explosion was on the down line to Fuengirola.'

'So we might expect any vehicle stolen between Tor-remolinos and there since one p.m. yesterday to be involved. Have we got the results of the forensic tests on the Fiat and the room in the Parador?'

'Varga has phoned to say he's got good latent prints from the hotel furniture and from the car doors. He's checking them out with Central Records now at the computer terminal in the *comisaría*. He'll be here to report later this morning.'

The scrambler phone sounded shrilly, and Navarro picked it up on the first long ring. He listened and then held his hand over the mouthpiece. 'It's Madrid, for you, Chief. The Head of the Anti-Terrorist Unit.'

Bernal made a wry grimace. 'He probably wants to know why I didn't get entirely blown up yesterday for the sake of the Fatherland.' Bernal took the instrument as if it were a poisonous asp. 'Comisario? Buenos días. No, I am still in one piece. Is there some news from the other resorts about the capture of the bombers?'

'I demand to know what you are up to, Bernal.' Navarro could hear the stentorian tones quite clearly. 'Why did you let those two *etarras* slip out of your grasp yesterday?'

'They evaded the Civil Guard cordon which I ordered as soon as we had recovered our breath after the explosion. They escaped along the railway line and probably took a

144

southbound train. At least we are pretty sure of their names, Comisario, and I hope to get confirmation shortly. We've put out a general alert along the coast.'

'It's not good enough, Bernal. And, what's more, I've been monitoring a stream of enquiries you've been making to Interpol about some missing youths. What on earth have they got to do with the Basque terrorist campaign? You must not waste time and resources on such unrelated matters.'

'I can't be certain that they aren't related,' replied Bernal guardedly. 'The abduction of foreign holidaymakers could be part of the *etarras*' attempt to destabilise the tourist trade. I fear the missing youths may have been murdered.'

'Leave it alone, Bernal. And that's an order. Let the local inspector handle it. I insist that you continue to follow my original instructions to concentrate all your resources on the terrorists' bombing campaign, is that clear?'

Navarro watched Bernal's face suffuse with blood and thought he was about to witness one of his chief's extremely rare outbursts of anger. But the voice that answered was cool and controlled: 'The Ministry's instructions will be fulfilled at all times. I don't need to remind you that the day-to-day management of my group is my responsibility alone. Is that clear to you, Comisario?'

'Just do as I have ordered,' expostulated the Head of the Anti-Terrorist Unit.

'The moment the Minister loses confidence in my command,' answered Bernal in a deadly voice, 'he will surely order my recall to Madrid.' He put the receiver back on its rest slowly.

'You didn't hang up on him, did you, *jefe*?' asked Navarro anxiously.

'I don't think so. Those spluttering noises must have been the scrambler device.' Bernal lit a Káiser and looked out at the peaceful scene: the holidaymakers were venturing back, albeit in smaller numbers than before, on to the beaches. 'Was that Palencia's decision, Paco?' He pointed down at the foreshore.

'No, Chief, it was the Chief of Police at Málaga, after consulting Madrid. The town councillors, hoteliers and shopkeepers have been screaming to the Ministry of Tourism about the damage to their trade. Since the entire beach has now been swept by metal-detectors and nothing has been found, Madrid has ordered the cordons to be removed, but the foot patrols by police and the Civil Guard are to be increased.'

'They've ordered this just when we had forced the *etarras* to switch from the beaches to the promenades and parks, where we might have had a better chance of spotting them,' Bernal mused. 'Why don't we ask for the co-operation of the public? We could put out leaflets in four or five languages asking people to report any suspicious behaviour or abandoned packages to the nearest policeman.'

'Palencia has gone to consult the Chief of Police about the possibility of making a public announcement, Chief.'

'It would be a good thing. Since the foreign newspapers are giving sensational accounts of the explosions, we must exploit the publicity. I take it there's been no press coverage of the missing foreign youths?'

'Not yet, but it could happen any moment.'

Bernal had a sudden thought. 'Get me Zurdo at Fuengirola, will you, Paco?'

Bernal's former trainee soon came on the line. 'Are you OK, Chief? I heard you were caught in yesterday's explosion at the Parador de Golf.'

'The reports of my injuries are much exaggerated, Zurdo. Have you had any trouble there yet?'

'No bombs, thank goodness. The Guardia Civil had patrols on these beaches almost from the moment the ultimatum was issued, so it's possible the *etarras* didn't have time to plant any. We're patrolling all the tourist places, naturally.'

'I think you should look into any cases of vehicles stolen in Fuengirola since yesterday at one p.m., Zurdo. If you consult your list of terrorist suspects, you'll find photographs of number 2874, Paxti Berástegui, and number 1342, Yolanda Aguirre. We're waiting for the fingerprint confirmation, but

146

I'm fairly sure these were the two who planted the bomb on the golf-course. They escaped along the railway, almost certainly taking the next train south. Palencia has sent his *cabo* to question the ticket inspector, who may have seen them getting on.'

'What makes you think they would have travelled to the end of the line at Fuengirola, Chief?'

'They could have got out at Torremolinos of course, but we radioed for a check on the single exit there, which is via an escalator. Since the other stations are all above ground and have manned ticket-barriers, Palencia thinks it more likely they would have stayed on until the terminus, where they could emerge in the thick of the passengers. If he's right, they would soon have tried to steal a vehicle, in order to carry on with their plans. Remember, they've changed their appearance considerably: the man is clean-shaven and short-haired now, and the woman has bleached her hair and she looks much older than on the mugshot.'

'Would they have been carrying the explosives and radio transmitter, Chief?'

'I suspect that somewhere they must have a cache to which they return for supplies from time to time.' Bernal looked at the wall-map of the province. 'I suggest you pay special attention to all the camping-sites in your area; a lot of comings and goings wouldn't be noticed in such a place. I'll ask the *comisario* at Marbella to check out the golf club at Río Real and the State Parador in the hills above Ojén.'

'OK, Chief, will do. I'll be back on the line as soon as there's any news.'

Bernal put down the phone and turned to Navarro. 'Where are the other members of our group, Paco?'

'Miranda and Lista are continuing with the enquiries at the hotels and *pensiónes*.'

'And Ángel and Elena?'

'They haven't called in yet, Chief. They went back to the Casa España in the early hours.'

'Call them all in for a conference at twelve-thirty, and ask

Varga to come as well. I'm going up to the *comisaría* to find Palencia.'

'Do you intend to go on with the stake-out in La Nogalera tonight, *jefe?*'

'Of course, in spite of that power-deranged chief in Madrid, who has ordered us to drop our enquiries into what are really the more sinister and important crimes.'

By the time Bernal returned to the Hotel Paraíso at noon, Varga had arrived with his reports.

'It's been confirmed, Chief,' said Navarro.

'What has?'

'The identity of the Basque couple,' said Varga. 'The latent prints I took from the abandoned Fiat and the wardrobe in the Parador match the prints held on Berta, the new central computer at the Escorial. The man is definitely Berástegui, and the woman is his girlfriend Yolanda. They are suspected of belonging to the Madrid commando that killed the two army officers last year.'

'Well done, Varga. Have you informed Madrid?' Bernal asked Navarro.

'Yes, Chief. And I've rung Zurdo at Fuengirola. He's given me this list of four vehicles stolen there since yesterday morning.'

Bernal read through the list, noting that it contained a red Renault 5 and two small SEATs all with Málaga *matrículas*, plus a Citroën van with a French registration.

'What else did you discover at the Parador?' Bernal asked the technician.

'Mainly that they must have assembled the bomb in the bedroom, Chief. There are traces of plastic explosive on the bedspread and the rug.'

'But there was no excess material in the boot of the car?'

'No, Chief. If there was any, they must have taken it with them, together with the radio transmitter. The desk-clerk remembers they had two large travel-bags with green-and-red Gucci-type trim.'

'I am more and more convinced they've got a cache they

can visiit to obtain the materials they need for each bomb,' commented Bernal.

Doctor Peláez now came in, looking as breezy as ever. 'Is there a coffee ready for me, Luis? I think I've earned a *carajillo* after cutting up that Civil Guard for you. Don't spare the drops of Cognac,' he said to Navarro.

'What did you find out, Peláez?'

'The Guard was felled by a commando-type blow to the throat, and then a second, fatal blow was delivered to the vagal nerve with the toe of a leather shoe. It's definitely another case of homicide.'

Navarro broke in. 'Inspector Ibáñez has sent us Berástegui's police record by telex, Chief. He was once trained as a GEO after doing his national service and he passed out top-grade in unarmed combat.'

'We must catch him,' said Bernal, 'before he kills again.'

Ángel Gallardo and Elena Fernández now arrived, looking, Bernal thought, like a pair of very with-it young holidaymakers.

'Are we going on with the stake-out tonight, *jefe*?' asked Ángel enthusiastically.

'Madrid has forbidden us to take part in the investigation into the missing teenagers, Ángel,' said Bernal. The young inspector looked crestfallen. 'But they don't know exactly what we're up to,' Bernal went on. 'I've discussed the matter with Palencia, who'll be coming back shortly, and we're all set to repeat the operation tonight. If Málaga or Madrid ask what we're planning, we've agreed to say it's an anti-terrorist operation to catch Berástegui and Aguirre.'

Bernal broke off as he noticed Elena Fernández staring as though transfixed at the photographs Navarro had pinned to the wall; he thought she had a look of near-terror on her face.

'What's wrong, Elena?'

'That Photofit, Chief.' She approached the wall slowly. 'Who is it meant to be?'

'Of course, you haven't seen it before. It was made up for us by the lodging-house keeper from the Paseo Marítimo of the stranger who came to collect the Italian boy's luggage.

149

Palencia has checked it out with the owner of the Casa España where you are staying, and he says it's a reasonable likeness, improbable as it seems.'

Elena's shoulders shook as she gazed at the dark face with the staring eyes.

'It's a bit unreal, isn't it?' commented Bernal. 'As though it's a character from a horror film.'

'No, Chief,' she said quietly. 'That's the spitting image of him.'

'But how did you manage to see him, Elena? He went to the Casa España when you weren't there.'

'It'll be her cat-man,' said Ángel laughing. 'She's got a thing about a fellow whom she's seen feeding the wild-cats on the rooftops of the Bajondillo after dark.'

Bernal looked into Elena's very frightened eyes. 'Are you sure he's the same man?'

'Yes, Chief, that's definitely him. I saw him again last night, just when you aborted the stake-out. Two municipal police-men stopped to chat to him in the new shopping-precinct, so, after he had gone, I questioned them. They said he's a South American who runs a relief agency for young people in distress.'

Bernal's interest suddenly sharpened. 'Young male for-eigners in distress?'

'They didn't say, but he helps drug-addicts and the like.'

'Did they tell you his name?'

'They didn't know it, but they said he's known as "The Angel of Torremolinos" because of all the work he saves them.'

'We must check him out at once. Did they know where he lives?'

'I asked them that. They think it's somewhere down in the Bajondillo.'

'Paco, get on to the chief of the municipal police and ask for their co-operation. Elena will point out which of his men she spoke to last night. We'll ask Palencia to check his files, too.' Bernal thought again about the cat-man. 'Could you see what he feeds the cats with, Elena?'

'It looks like the most disgusting offal, all stringy and dripping blood.' She looked at her chief and shivered suddenly. 'You don't think—'

'He must be disposing of the bodies somehow. There's been no sign of the five missing youths, or of their remains, and it's the hardest thing in the world to dispose of corpses and leave no trace. What do you think, Peláez?'

The doctor's gleaming countenance became animated. 'There have been cases of dismemberment in which the pieces have been fed to domestic or farm animals, Bernal. I remember a case in Cuenca—'

'Spare us the grisly details, Doctor. But those wild-cats on the roof, would that be feasible?'

Peláez looked doubtful. 'The entrails, perhaps, but not the major bones. Now, if the animals were hungry Alsatians, or pigs—'

Elena went white and sat down in a chair. Bernal hastened to prevent more of the pathologist's revelations. 'We need samples of that offal he throws to the cats for you to test. What do you think, Varga? Could it be arranged without his cottoning on?'

'The inspectors will have to show me the spot in the daylight first, sir. The cats may be rabid, so I'll have to get protective clothing.'

'What time does he usually feed them, Elena?' asked Bernal.

'After dark, Chief, when most of the tourists have gone to dine; about nine to nine-thirty.'

'We must try to obtain a sample without the suspect realising,' said Bernal. 'Then Lista and Miranda can follow him and find out where he lives. I don't want him frightened, or we may never find the bodies of his victims.'

'It must be somewhere remote, or surely a neighbour would have noticed the smell in this heat,' said Ángel, causing Elena to shudder once more.

'That's why I asked Miranda and Lista yesterday to enquire about empty premises or garages,' said Bernal. 'The place must be far from easy discovery, and yet near at hand,

151

because there's no sign he uses a vehicle, is there, Elena?'

'No, Chief; he couldn't do in those narrow lanes.'

'We'll consult Palencia, because he was born and bred here and should know of any likely places.'

By 1.30 p.m. Navarro had persuaded Bernal to return to Cabo Pino for lunch and a siesta before the two operations now planned for the evening and night. The Superintendent asked the police driver to return for him at 7.30 sharp. When he made his way wearily up to the duplex apartment, he found Consuelo and her sister-in-law in the kitchen making up a picnic-basket.

'We're taking the children for a boat-trip, Luchi. We thought it would be safer than going to the beach. Are you coming with us?'

'Where are the children now?'

'Down in the village shop buying a melon and any other fruit they fancy.'

'I think I'd better rest here, Chelo. We've got a big operation planned for this evening.'

'Shall I make you a French omelette and a mixed salad?'

'No, don't keep the children waiting. I'll stroll down to the quay with you and get something in the yacht club. I hope you've hired a decent-sized boat.'

'The next-door neighbour has very kindly offered to take us in his launch. It's got a canopy, so I shan't get burnt by the sun.'

'And the children can swim off the rocks round the point,' said the sister-in-law. 'They're fed up with the crowds in the swimming-pool, now the beach is unsafe.'

'Let's get going,' said Bernal. 'The kids will be getting impatient.'

Bernal stood on the small jetty and watched as they boarded the quite substantial launch, which had a small cabin, and waved as it sped out of the new marina. He turned into the bar of the yacht club and loosened his silk tie. He decided he needed a *doble* of the local beer, whatever it tasted like.

★   ★   ★

Inspectora Elena Fernández took Varga the technician into the Casa España, in the doorway of which the owner's wife smiled knowingly as her beautiful young lodger led the stocky dark-haired stranger up to her room. Really, these modern Spanish girls! They were no better than the foreign girls they had criticised for so many years. Taking him up to her room, and before lunch, too!

Elena ignored Anna's complacent smile and Albert's lascivious leer, and took Varga through the patio and up the outside staircase to her bedroom.

'You can see most of the roof opposite from this balcony, Varga.'

The mangy cats of many different hues were now snoozing contentedly in the shade of the chimney-pots.

'There's nowhere to hide, apart from behind those chimneys, Inspectora.'

'What about the roof of the Red Lion? It overlooks the spot where he distributes the offal.'

'That's a possibility,' Varga admitted, 'but I'd have to use a line and grappling-hook to try to get a piece or two before the cats eat it all.'

'After the man's gone of course. Otherwise he'd notice.'

'I'll go over and talk to the owner of the pub. We'll need his co-operation.'

Elena looked up and down the lane. 'There's not much cover for Lista and Miranda, is there?'

'The real problem is forecasting how your cat-man leaves the rooftop after feeding the cats. There could be a way of climbing down to the cottages on the far side.'

'It would be best if I have a transceiver tuned to the same pre-set frequency as Lista's and Miranda's. If Lista stays out of sight at the bottom of the lane at the junction by the Britannia, and Miranda waits at the Windmill restaurant at the top of the Bajondillo, I can tell them which way he goes.'

'And if he goes over the top and gets away on the other side? I'd better have a radio, too, to tell Lista to go round the block in search of him.'

Elena agreed, and Varga took his leave. She watched him cross the crowded lane and enter the Red Lion. Despite the muggy heat Elena shivered as she watched the cats licking themselves, as though waiting for their next helping of human entrails. She must keep a grip on her feelings, she told herself. It wouldn't do for her male colleagues to see her panicking. But the memory of the staring eyes of the cat-man obsessed her, and filled both her waking and sleeping moments.

Superintendent Luis Bernal woke with a start and groped for his watch on the bedside table. It was nearly 7.30 p.m., and Consuelo and her family hadn't returned. He got up and went to the balcony. The enormous setting sun threw a glorious blaze across the dark-grey watery horizon. The marina looked to be full of boats, but from that distance he couldn't pick out the neighbour's large launch.

Bernal decided to get ready for the evening's operations and wet-shaved in the bathroom. By 7.50 he began to get worried about Consuelo's late return. He would go down to the jetty and make some enquiries. The remaining red sunlight was cut off now by the rocky point from the small clump of date-palms below the apartments. At first the resultant contrasting shade did not allow him to discern clearly the man and woman getting out of a small red car parked in the tunnel that stretched from the approach road under the main apartment-block to the quay. Bernal paused in the doorway of the duplex and let his eyes become adjusted to the growing dusk.

A blonde woman accompanied by a dark-haired man carrying a travel-bag now emerged. He stood back out of their sight, observing their somewhat furtive progress past the palm-fronded park. They appeared to be making for the yacht club, where the garish strings of coloured lights had been switched on. Immediately in front of it was an ornamental arid garden of rocks and cactuses, where he saw the couple stop and sit down.

As soon as their backs were turned, Bernal slipped out of his doorway and went to the short road-tunnel to inspect the car they had illegally parked there. He saw it was a Renault 5,

and the Málaga registration rang a bell: it was surely one of
the vehicles stolen from Fuengirola the previous day. Inside
on the floor he could see what appeared to be a portable
radio in a green–camouflage bag. Was it a transmitter? He
tried the passenger-door, but it was locked. Moving rapidly
to the driver's door, he found he was in luck. Looking round
to make sure he was not being observed, Bernal opened the
door softly and picked up the heavy piece of apparatus. It
definitely seemed to be a radio transmitter.

Moving now with urgency, Bernal returned to the duplex
and let himself in. From the window he could see the couple
crouched over one of the rocks in the arid garden. He turned
to examine his prize: it was a heavy transmitter of Czech
manufacture. He picked up the phone and called Navarro.

'Get me Zurdo at Fuengirola at fast as you can, Paco. I've
spotted the Basque couple. They're planting a bomb in the
small garden in front of the yacht club here. If Zurdo gets
his act together quickly, he can trap them. There's only one
road out of Cabo Pino, and he's only six kilometres away.'

'Shouldn't you warn the customers in the club, Chief?'

'No, it would give the game away, and in any case I've got
the radio transmitter they'd need to set the bomb off.'

Bernal went back to the balcony to check that the *etarra*
suspects were still occupied in their task. The phone rang
almost immediately, and Zurdo came on the line.

'I've sent a squad of GEOs, and two jeeps of Civil Guards
are on their way, Chief.'

Bernal explained carefully the approaches to the spot.
'You must seal off the exit to the tunnel and place a further
cordon up the hill below the main N340.'

'What are they doing now, Chief?'

'They're sitting on a rock pretending to make love whenever anyone passes by. They're obviously not in a hurry.'

'I'm on my way.'

A further thought struck Bernal. 'For goodness' sake warn
the coastguard patrol, Zurdo. The bombers may try to get
away in a boat once they find out they're trapped. Also you'd
better close off the beach approach from the south-west in

case they make off along the foreshore. There's a long stretch of dunes with sparse pine trees further inland that could give them some cover.'

'Don't worry, Chief. We'll soon have Cabo Pino totally sealed off.'

Bernal went into the children's room and found what he wanted: a pair of small binoculars. Returning to the balcony he trained the glasses on the garden of the yacht club. There were no passers-by now, and the suspects were obviously busy hiding something under one of the ornamental rocks.

A powerful launch with its headlight and navigational lamps lit entered the harbour and moored at the jetty. The Basque pair stopped what they were doing and sat with their arms round each other, pretending to be a courting couple. Bernal focused the weak prismatics on to the launch. Oh God, it was Consuelo, her sister-in-law and the children returning. Where had they been so late? He watched with a feeling of horrified helplessness as they strolled past the pair of terrorists and emerged on to the esplanade. Soon they were nearing the apartment and wishing a cheerful goodnight to the neighbour who had navigated them. Bernal hurried down to meet them in the hall.

'Don't put the lights on yet, Chelo. Take the children into the back bedroom.'

'What's wrong, Luis? Is it a bomb threat?'

'What makes you think that?'

'I'm suspicious of that couple we passed by the garden of the yacht club.'

'Why are you?'

'Well, whoever saw a courting couple with the man holding a spade with a broken-off handle? Are they planting a bomb down there?' She joined him on the darkened balcony.

'I'm certain of it.'

'I'll stay with my sister-in-law and the children at the back, and you'd better get away from that window.'

'Don't worry, the GEOs are on their way, and I've got the remote-control device they were going to use here.'

156

He pointed at the dressing-table. 'The bomb can't go off without that.'

Out of the corner of his eye he saw a sudden movement in the mouth of the road-tunnel. Then a line of dark-uniformed men with blackened faces and wearing balaclava helmets just emerged from the darkness.

'Come and watch, if you like.'

Further along the shore to the south-west, they could see jeeps approaching through the sand-dunes, and in the bay two fast patrol-boats rounded the point at speed and made for the harbour.

'It's zero hour, Chelo.'

They watched with bated breath as the pair of terrorists sprang to their feet and started to make for the stolen car parked in the road-tunnel. Then, as they caught sight of the line of now running GEOs, the man pulled out a gun and, clutching the woman by the arm, started dragging her towards the beach. When two Civil Guard jeeps with headlights on full beam topped the last line of sand-dunes, the couple turned back desperately towards the marina where the two coastguard patrol-boats had stopped engines just outside the line of moored yachts.

Cornered now, the male terrorist pointed his pistol towards the arid garden and fired all its contents at the rock. There was a blinding yellow flash followed by a whooshing sound and a deafening explosion, the blast of which threw Luis and Consuelo on to the bed.

'I thought you said it couldn't go off,' she said accusingly.

'I didn't plan on his doing that! It must have been a lucky shot.'

Consuelo dragged herself to her feet and went to the balcony. 'Not so lucky. I think they've both had it. I hope no one's been killed in the yacht club; it seems to be badly damaged.'

Pandemonium had now broken out as all the inhabitants emerged in alarm and the GEOs and Civil Guards converged on the scene. Sirens and bells of approaching ambulances and fire-engines could be heard.

'I'd better find Zurdo and tell him to sort all this out,' said Bernal. 'I've got to go to work.'

'Go to work?' echoed Consuelo incredulously. 'What do you call this?'

'The serious case still hasn't been cracked, Chelo.'

At 9.30 p.m. the tall, powerfully built stranger emerged from his curious dwelling and made for the Bajondillo carrying a plastic-wrapped parcel that was much larger than usual. There'd be a special treat for his wild-cats tonight, he thought, even though he hadn't been able to cut it up for them, but they had razor-sharp fangs and would soon tear it apart.

He stopped at the junction in the lane near the Britannia pub, from which the noise of rowdy singing emerged. Suddenly he had the feeling of being watched, just as he had on the previous night in La Nogalera. He stood uncertainly in a shadowy doorway and looked carefully up the lane towards the town; he could see no one. His gaze scanned all the windows in the narrow street; he saw nothing to cause him alarm. Partially reassured, he moved boldly out into the lamplight once more and began to climb the steps from the Bajondillo.

Elena Fernández stood shivering in the soft evening breeze – she knew not whether from cold or from fear – behind the shabby pink curtains of her darkened window. From her vantage-point she had a good view of the occasional passers-by. The trumpet being practised by the boy who lived in one of the houses below the Casa España wailed lugubrious jazz that was hopelessly out of tune. How that sound had got on her nerves during the past three days!

Speaking in a whisper, Elena checked that the transceiver was working that connected her to Varga, who was perched on the roof of the Red Lion opposite, and to her colleagues Lista and Miranda. Bernal, Navarro and Ángel Gallardo, she knew, were in the office in the Hotel Paraíso listening in on the same frequency. The Chief had insisted that Ángel be kept out of sight during this preliminary operation, in order not to jeopardise his key rôle in the stake-out still planned for the early hours.

Bernal had decided that they must first establish where the cat-man lived and whether the offal he threw to the cats was of human origin; then they could proceed to get a judicial order to search his house and take him in for questioning. If the result was positive, Ángel could be saved from possible danger in the stake-out plan. Of course it would be better if they could catch him *in flagrante delicto*, but Bernal never wished to put the lives of his colleagues at unnecessary risk.

The radio Elena was holding now sprang to life. 'Lista here. Possible suspect just turned into the Bajondillo carrying large parcel.'

Elena strained to see the man among the moving shadows cast by the swinging lanterns further down the lane. Then she saw the dreaded tall figure striding towards her and she shrank back instinctively into the comparative safety of her room. Peering between the crack in the curtains, she saw his face more clearly now in the light streaming out through the windows of the Red Lion. As she recognised those pitiless staring eyes, the man paused, then gazed straight up at her window; Elena staggered back in shock. He was looking at her window, only hers, as though expecting to find her there! Now he began to unwrap the large package, glancing furtively up and down the cobbled street. When he was sure there was no one in sight, he vaulted over the railings with incredible agility and landed on the roof-tiles, where the wild-cats started to screech and claw at his legs. Elena could hear him talking to them soothingly in a low voice while he removed the last of the wrappings and threw down what appeared to be a sizeable ham.

The cats rapaciously attacked their dead prey as the man seemed to watch them with satisfaction, since he patted the backs of one or two of them as they vied with one another to join the feast.

Elena managed to whisper into the transceiver: 'Identification positive. He's on the roof feeding the cats.'

Again she shrank back, shivering as he looked up at her balcony; there could be no doubt that it was hers he was interested in, since he didn't spare a glance for the others. Elena almost stopped breathing. When she dared look out once more, he had completely vanished. She put her head right through the drawn curtains and looked up and down the street. There was no one at all to be seen.

'Varga here. Keep out of sight, Inspectora. He's crouching behind the chimney-pots.'

Elena quickly withdrew her head. Thank heaven, there was a strong evening breeze that continually blew the curtains; with luck he wouldn't have noticed her movement. Holding her breath in fearful anticipation, Elena suddenly heard a clatter of tiles. The radio cracked.

'Varga here. He's away! Across the roof and down a drain-pipe on the wall of one of the lower cottages. I'm trying to obtain the sample now.'

Elena summoned up enough courage to peep out; she saw the shadow of Varga tossing a line down from the roof of the Red Lion. The grappling-hook hit the pantiles with a light metallic clatter that temporarily disturbed the animals gorging on the carrion.

'Lista here. I'm doubling back along the lower lane to spot him coming out.'

Elena watched in trepidation as Varga leant precariously over the eaves and kept throwing the line without catching the piece of meat, causing the cats to scatter in alarm on each occasion. At last he got a good hold and began to haul the meat up while the frustrated animals screamed and leapt in an attempt to recover it. Soon it was beyond their reach, but Elena feared they would find a way of jumping on to the much higher roof to attack Varga.

Miranda now came on the radio: 'I'm coming down to assist Lista.'

The starving wild-cats were now sharpening their claws in vain on the whitewashed side-wall of the Red Lion, though two or three of their more intelligent brethren were trying to climb a drainpipe that ran down from the point where Varga was stashing his prize into a large black plastic bag. He must be quick, thought Elena. Then she saw him disappear behind the chimneys of the pub and knew he would get down through a fanlight on the far side.

'Varga here. Coming in now, Chief.'

The howling of the cats reached a new pitch as they seemed to sense that their food had been snatched from them. After a few minutes had passed, Elena saw the technician leave the pub, shouting a cheery goodnight to the landlord, and start walking out of the Bajondillo towards the base of the cliff where he would take the lift from the hotel garage up to Bernal's office. Elena knew there was a police car waiting to take Varga to the path. lab in Málaga where Doctor Peláez was waiting to run tests on the piece of offal.

Once the sample had been successfully obtained, their orders were to keep the suspect under close surveillance without alarming him. Elena looked up the Cuesta del Tago and saw Miranda coming down quickly, keeping in the shadow of the walls. Lista spoke on the radio.

'I've spotted him. I'm at the corner of the lane that runs parallel with the Paseo Marítimo. Suspect now approaching from the small group of fishermen's cottages under the cliff.'

Miranda glanced up at Elena's window as he passed, then he hastened to the doorway of the Britannia at the bottom of the lane. Elena began to ask herself why the cat-man hadn't jumped back over the railings; but, then, he had vanished in the same manner when she and Ángel had observed him on the first occasion. She hoped he wouldn't turn up the lane again; she really couldn't bear the prospect of his stopping under her window. She felt for her service pistol to give herself some badly needed confidence.

There was absolutely no sign of Miranda. Had he entered the lower pub to keep watch from a window, or was he hidden in the small yard at the side of it? She couldn't tell. Some young holidaymakers now emerged from the Red Lion opposite her; they began to hoot and skylark as they made their way up to the town. The normality of their high spirits helped to steady her nerve. Should she follow Miranda and join in the shadowing operation? But Bernal had told her to stay put on the balcony until further orders. After all, Lista and Miranda were the most expert of the group in following suspects without being observed. They would interchange with each other, one stopping in a doorway while the other overtook him, in case the suspect backtracked. She knew they had a well-developed and discreet system of signalling to each other without needing to use their transceivers, which were so cumbersome and treacherous. Certainly they were now preserving complete radio silence.

Bernal sat chain-smoking with Inspector Palencia in the office, listening to the brief radio messages amplified on a loudspeaker.

'I hope he doesn't cotton on to the fact that he's being followed, Palencia.'

'I wish you'd let me take part, Comisario.'

'It would be too risky. He may have seen you and your men going in and out of the police station.'

Ángel stood staring out of the window as though hoping to see what was happening in the darkness far below, while Navarro sat reading the reports on his desk without taking in the contents. Waiting was the toughest part of a policeman's work – and the greater part of it – which the gangster films never revealed. At last the radio sprang into life.

'Lista here. He's gone into an old house beyond the carpark of the Bajondillo Apartments. It's the third house on the right on the old road that leads diagonally up to the top of the Avenida del Lido.'

Bernal stepped over to the wall-plan accompanied by Palencia.

'The street's called the Camino de Marcelo,' said the local inspector, pointing to the place.

Bernal went over to the microphone. 'Lista? Bernal. Is there any way of getting round the back?'

'It doesn't seem so, Chief. The house backs into the cliff and there's no side-entrance.'

'You and Miranda had better stay there and follow him if he comes out again.' Bernal turned back to Palencia. 'Let's obtain a search-warrant for that house.'

'I'll go round to the judge of instruction, Comisario.'

'We oughtn't to arrest the suspect unless Doctor Peláez gets a positive result on the sample, but that's going to take an hour or two. We should get egg on our faces if we brought him in when he's only an eccentric cat-lover.' Bernal looked at his watch. 'It's nearly ten-fifteen. If we're going to mount the stake-out in La Nogalera by twelve-thirty, we'd better make sure everyone gets some food into them. Paco, tell Lista and Miranda to take it in turns to get a snack in the nearest bar, then you can order some sandwiches and beer to be sent up to us. Elena had better come in now.'

By 10.45 p.m., in the path. lab of the military hospital at Málaga, Doctor Peláez and the local police pathologist were carefully unwrapping Varga's grisly catch, while Bernal's chief technician went to the canteen for some supper. The local doctor made a face when he smelt the putre-fying object, whereas Peláez showed no sign of noticing the stench.

'It's the right side of a pelvis with part of the launch, wouldn't you say, Doctor?' The local man agreed. 'Let's take some slide specimens and then we can dissect it fully.'

Nothing stirred in the dark street. Lista could hear the rhythm of flamenco dancing coming from one of the beach establishments and the muffled roar of the breakers beyond. From above him, to the south-west, came the tuneless wailing of a jazz-trumpeter.

Lista had seen a light go on when the suspect entered the house in the Camino de Marcelo, but now it was in com-plete darkness. Presumably he was in one of the back rooms, perhaps taking his evening meal. The inspector sat patiently under a tree on the grassy plot at the end of the lane; he hoped Miranda would relieve him soon.

*   *   *

It was 11.10 when Doctor Peláez rang from Málaga, and Navarro handed the phone to Bernal.

'The specimen has been dead for some weeks – it's impossible to say exactly how many, because it was refrigerated at an early stage. It's been defrosted recently and is beginning to putrefy. I've sent Varga back to you with my typed report.'

'But what else can you tell me, Peláez? Can you confirm it's human? And is it male or female?'

'It's probably male, but not human of course. I thought you knew that. It's half the pelvis and part of the right femur of a good example of *Caprum hispanicum* – one of our native goats, and about three years old, I'd say.'

'A goat?' repeated Bernal in astonishment. 'How would he have come by that? Do the butchers sell goat's meat?'

'This one's been properly skinned and hung, and professionally cut up, Luis. And some butchers do sell it, especially in the country districts. Surely you must have tried *churrasco de choto* in the Madrid restaurants?'

'For my ulcer's sake, I'm glad to say I haven't.'

After thanking Peláez, Bernal turned to Palencia. 'We daren't execute that search-warrant for the moment. If the cat-man is really the killer of the foreign youths, he isn't serving them up to his cats, or he hasn't done so tonight at any rate.'

'Shall we proceed with the stake-out, then?'

'There's no other way I can think of, even if it takes a fortnight.'

The scrambler phone rang peremptorily, and Navarro snatched it up. 'Yes, Comisario. I'll just see if he's still in the building.' Navarro looked enquiringly at Bernal and mouthed the word 'Madrid'.

'I'll take it, Paco. Buenas noches, Comisario. Is there any news for us?'

'Zurdo did extremely well at Cabo Pino, Bernal. He caught two of them in the act, though only the woman Yolanda is still alive for us to question. That is, if she survives. They've taken her to the *UVI* at Marbella hospital.'

164

'Were there any civilian casualties, Comisario?' Bernal asked, knowing the answer very well.

'Some minor cuts from flying glass in the yacht club, that's all. I shall personally see to it that Zurdo gets a special commendation and a press mention. But more to the point: are you making any progress at all in Torremolinos?'

Bernal gulped and then decided to let his former trainee take all the credit. 'Zurdo's an excellent officer. He seems to have handled the operation brilliantly.' Bernal stopped to light a Káiser. 'I think we may conclude that the two who laid the bomb at the Parador de Golf are the same as the pair Zurdo trapped at Cabo Pino. But I beg you to order a complete press blackout on the Cabo Pino affair for forty-eight hours. That would give us a chance to trace their accomplices and find their arms cache. Meanwhile we are maintaining the strictest vigilance here, you can be sure.'

'Very well. I agree to the press ban, but I hope your group will do better than it has up until now.'

Bernal said nothing as he put down the phone, but he realised that the others had heard some, if not all, of his interlocutor's remarks.

'We'll press on with our plan, Palencia, without informing either Málaga or Madrid. You'll only get a case like this once in a lifetime.'

Soon after midnight the squads of plain-clothes men took up their positions in La Nogalera, while Bernal, as on the previous night, went up to the office above the travel agency that commanded the square. Palencia and he had been obliged to regroup their men into four squads, because of Lista and Miranda's assignment at the suspect's house, but at least they would now have the advantage of being informed as soon as he set out from the Camino de Marcelo.

Bernal had decided to dispense with Elena's 'offended girlfriend' routine, in order to place her directly in charge of one of the squads in the first-floor restaurant at the entrance to the shopping-precinct.

At 12.40 a.m., Miranda and Lista, who were stationed strategically a hundred metres apart, observed the suspect emerge from his house, where he stood on the threshold as though sniffing the air. They waited to see which way he would turn. The tall stranger lit a cigarette, looked up and down the street, and then went off northwards up the Camino de Marcelo. From behind the tree opposite, Lista let him gain some twenty-five metres before radioing in.

'Lista here. He's heading north towards the Avenida del Lido. We're following.'

Bernal knew that only he, Navarro and Miranda could listen in to this message, since the radios of the plain-clothes squads in the square were tuned to a different frequency. Bernal pressed the button on his large set for that frequency and called Ángel Gallardo: 'He's started out, Ángel. Get into position.' Then Bernal called Navarro at the Hotel Paraíso. 'Paco, when he reaches the Avenida del Lido, tell Varga and his assistant to go in.'

The tall, powerfully built stranger was deeply troubled. Something was wrong; he had felt it since the previous night. That girl in the Casa España, why was she spying on him? She had been in the shopping-precinct on her own during the early hours, and now this very evening he had caught a glimpse of her silly white face peering through the drawn curtains of her darkened room. He felt a rising violent hatred of her; perhaps he would have to put a stop to her prying into his affairs.

The man stopped frequently to look back. He still had the sensation of being followed, and whenever he turned it always seemed as though a rapid movement had quickly ceased, yet he never actually saw anyone. It was most aggravating. He decided to outfox whoever it was: he would go the long way round, past the Hotel Cervantes and up to the Calle San Miguel that way. The road was long and wide, with no cover; if anyone were following him, he would be sure to spot them and he could then mingle with the people in the Plaza de la Costa del Sol and double back into La Nogalera from the north side.

Bernal listened with some dismay to Lista and Miranda's brief whispered messages. The cat-man was showing signs of nervousness at being followed, and on the Calle de las Mercedes where he now was there was virtually no cover, there being high walls on each side with very few entrances before the Hotel Cervantes. He ordered them to stay back. Navarro from the front window of the Hotel Paraíso would be able to observe the suspect's approach, and Palencia, who was in charge of the first plain-clothes squad at the corner of San Miguel, would pick him up from there.

Bernal had a third frequency-setting on his radio set to which only Navarro, Varga and he had access, and he was anxiously waiting for a message on that. At last it came.

'Varga to Chief. We're in.'

At last the tall stranger was satisfied: no one at all had followed him up the empty wide stretches of the Calle de las Mercedes. He stopped to light a cigarette outside the entrance to the Hotel Paraíso, unaware he was being watched by Navarro.

The tall stranger now passed the small clump of trees where the Moroccan drug-dealers hung out; how he hated those vultures who preyed on the frailty of weak-willed young people. Such types had been the cause of his younger brother's downfall, which in turn had broken their mother's heart, quite literally, bringing about her early death. He must continue to punish these young offenders for their wickedness; it was his allotted task – divinely inspired, he had been assured of that, even in the mission. He had done his best in Montevideo, but they had started spying on him and prying into his secrets. How right he had been to take a berth in that merchant ship bound for Málaga, though it had cost him all his meagre savings, for here he had discovered a real witches' cauldron of unspeakable vices, which threatened at times to overwhelm him. How could he, singlehanded, clean up these tents of wickedness? Yet he must be selective and do his small part in reducing the general burden of sin.

Bernal listened carefully to Navarro's brief radio reports on the movements of the suspect from Las Mercedes to San Miguel, and passed the information to Palencia. Then he heard the local inspector announcing that his squad had spotted the cat-man entering San Miguel. Here there were still a number of passers-by, and so many shop doorways that the team had a relatively easy task.

From his vantage-point, Bernal could see that Ángel Gallardo was now in position near the large magnolia tree opposite one of the terrace-bars that had already closed for the night. Elena Fernández would have the best view of him from the first floor of the restaurant.

Suddenly the third frequency on Bernal's radio came live.

'Varga to Chief: we haven't found anything incriminating so far. There are some papers in a desk about the founding of a mission to save young people from vice with an address in Montevideo. There's also a Uruguayan passport in the name of Héctor Malinsky, born in Artigas on the fifteenth of January 1941; profession: member of the Order of Jesus.'

'Give me the passport number, Varga, and Navarro will send it to Interpol. Is there any sign of the bodies?'

'Nothing, Chief. My assistant's just found a large deep-freeze cabinet in the back kitchen. We'll check that out at once.'

'We'll give you plenty of warning if the suspect shows signs of returning, Varga. Over and out.'

Bernal had not revealed to Palencia his decision to send in Varga secretly to search the suspect's house. That would protect the young officer should there be an official complaint made later on. Bernal felt he must have something, just one tiny piece of physical evidence, to connect the cat-man with at least one of the missing youths. Then he could bring him in for lengthy questioning. Without that it was stalemate: he could keep Malinsky under constant surveillance, but he could not prove he had anything to do with the disappearance of the foreign tourists.

As he surveyed the almost deserted square where the *regadores* had got out the thick hoses to sluice down the pavements and terraces, Bernal realised that, because of the need of Palencia's squad to follow the suspect up San Miguel, that corner of La Nogalera had been left unguarded. He called Lista and Miranda on the second frequency and told them to station themselves on the east side of the square until the suspect reappeared.

Bernal took up the powerful Japanese night-glasses and swept them over the scene. There was a group of young foreigners singing on the grass nearest the airline office below him, and there were four or five more figures among the trees, probably taking drugs. Ángel had stationed himself on the same grassy plot as these, but somewhat apart from them, pretending to be asleep with his head resting on a small rucksack that contained his pistol and his transmitter. He had a tiny remote-control microphone under his T-shirt.

The second frequency came on the air. 'Palencia here. He's leaving the Plaza Costa del Sol and is making for La Nogalera.'

Bernal peered down at the side-street below him and soon had the binoculars trained on the suspect. At once he understood Elena's earlier reactions to this man. The Photofit picture, melodramatic as it had seemed, was really a good likeness in that it caught the crazed look in the eyes so well. As he assessed the tall figure with its powerful physique, Bernal felt as though he had known him before, known he was present in that place committing his crimes. He represented a challenge to be taken up, and then overcome. Now he had the suspect in a trap. Would he fall for the bait Bernal had provided?

Elena Fernández did not need binoculars to spot the presence of the cat-man, or to hear the Chief's warning message to Ángel. She felt the evil of the man's presence like a physical wound. Why did this criminal get under her skin so? For she had no doubt of his guilt; she had intuited it from that first night when she had seen him on the rooftops of the Bajondillo. Now she watched him stroll quietly across the square, avoiding the fierce jets of water unleashed by the *regadores* who, as real *aguafiestas* or spoilsports, had broken up the singing party at the western end of La Nogalera.

Elena tensed as the suspect came to where Ángel was now sitting up, mixing what appeared to be smack on a small sheet of tinfoil which he heated up by lighting a series of matches. He sniffed the mixture vigorously up each nostril as the cat-man stopped to watch. The suspect moved off towards the entrance to the shopping-precinct immediately below the place from where she kept vigil, and Elena drew back out of sight. Would he leave the square altogether? He had stopped again, this time to light a cigarette; he was turning to observe Ángel's activities from a distance. The young inspector, wearing a very fetching silver-and-white T-shirt and white slacks, had now stretched out again with his head on his rucksack and a beatific smile on his handsome countenance. Could the suspect resist the bait? All the police watchers held their breath.

At last the tall stranger turned back towards the square looking about him carefully, and then jumped on to the grassy plot and sat down at Ángel's side. The trap was closing, and all the watchers could listen in to the conversation if one developed.

But nothing happened. The man sat smoking, occasionally glancing down at the young man at his side. After a while Ángel pretended to stir and turn sideways, and then went back to sleep. The stranger slipped his hand into the left side-pocket of Ángel's jeans, but found only a small bundle of banknotes which he carefully replaced.

The *regadores* were now dragging their hoses towards the east side of the square, while Bernal watched them anxiously, in case they spoiled the pick-up. But he needn't have worried: the stranger nudged Ángel gently in the arm and said: 'Hey, you're going to get soaked if you don't move from here!'

Ángel feigned extreme sleepiness and attempted to open one eye. 'Who're you?'

170

'They call me "The Angel of Torremolinos". I help people like you to stay out of trouble.'

Ángel tried to sit up, and the stranger put a solicitous arm under his shoulder.

'What a coincidence!' the Inspector mumbled. 'I'm your double!'

Bernal hoped that Ángel wouldn't overdo his act.

'What do you mean?' asked the stranger suspiciously, leaving go Ángel's arm.

The young inspector slumped comfortably back on to the rucksack. 'I'm Ángel, too, on holiday in Torremolinos!'

The tall stranger seemed to grasp the import of Ángel's slurred speech and laughed. 'We're both angels, then. How confusing!' He pulled out a packet of cigarettes. 'Do you smoke?'

'No, thanks, not tobacco. I smoked two *porros* earlier.'

The tall stranger smiled, and thought grimly: This one's just like the German youth, Keller. 'Where are you staying?'

'Down there somewhere.' Ángel pointed vaguely towards the sea. 'At a boarding-house on the cliff-path.'

The spray of water expertly directed by the *regadores* came much closer to where they sat.

'Come on. I'll take you back.' Ángel allowed himself to be hoisted to his feet, swaying as though drunk. 'I'll carry your rucksack if you like.'

Ángel was suddenly concerned at having taken from him his service pistol and the radio on which his hidden microphone depended for transmitting this conversation to Bernal, but he thought it unwise to protest. The tall stranger helped him down on to the pavement and led him towards the entrance to the shopping-precinct.

Bernal watched anxiously as the four squads stationed round the square began to converge on the suspect; they were moving in much too fast, he judged. He saw Elena emerge from the door of the restaurant just as Malinsky turned his head and caught sight of her. He grabbed Ángel in a powerful grip and began to run, dragging him along.

171

Bernal spoke urgently into the radio. 'He's spotted the tails and Elena. He's running into the precinct.'

Ángel struggled to free himself, and they heard him shout: 'Hey, man! Let me go. What are you doing?'

The next moment they had both vanished and the radio went silent.

They've blown it, thought Bernal bitterly, just when it was going so well. He called Navarro on the open frequency. 'Bernal here. All units must give top priority to freeing Inspector Gallardo and arresting Malinsky.'

Elena shrank back into the doorway of the restaurant as she realised the suspect had recognised her. Then she heard Bernal's general order, and told her four plain-clothes men to follow the suspect and his hostage. Hers was the nearest squad and should overtake them quickly. She ran into the well-lit precinct, but could see no one. Two of her men started looking into every doorway as she and the other two went running down the curving street. When they reached the Vaca Sentada steak-bar, Elena saw the two municipal policemen of the previous night.

'Have you seen that man I asked you about? The Angel of Torremolinos?'

'No, Inspectora, he hasn't come past us tonight.'

'But he must have done! He's dragging one of our colleagues with him.'

'I'm afraid we haven't seen them.'

Elena ran back, just as one of the municipal men started to say something. She met Lista and Miranda, who had joined in the search, but of the two Angels there was no sign.

Bernal turned up the volume on the first frequency to try to hear something form Ángel Gallardo's hidden microphone, but there was only loud static. He spoke to Navarro on the closed third frequency. 'The suspect's broken loose with Ángel as hostage. Warn Varga to get clear of the house at once.'

Bernal saw Palencia and his squad running across the grassy plot, and he tried to make contact: 'Palencia? Bernal here. How could the suspect have got away from that precinct?'

The radio crackled, and Palencia came on. 'There's an old alleyway at the back of the shops that comes out at La Fuente restaurant. I'll take my squad round the back to Calle Roca and cut them off.'

This message was also heard by the other squads, and Lista soon found the narrow entrance to the alley.

'Come on,' he shouted to Miranda, 'this way! You go back with your squad, Elena, and get to La Fuente before he does.'

Lista and Miranda hared along the dark lane which was lit only by an occasional pool of light from a window, while the third squad followed them more slowly, stopping to examine every doorway and entrance.

Bernal spoke to Navarro on the closed frequency. 'Has Varga got out?'

'Yes, Chief, he's leaving now.'

'Tell him to stay outside with his assistant and call us for assistance if Malinsky returns to his house. Have you tried to contact Ángel on the radio?'

'His set's completely dead. Perhaps Malinsky dropped the rucksack as he fled.'

'We'll search for it later.'

After a four-minute run, Lista and Miranda reached the tiny La Fuente square where three lanes converged, and bumped into a breathless Elena. At that moment Palencia and his squad came running in from the Calle de Roca.

'He's eluded us,' said Palencia, crestfallen.

'He can't have got far dragging Gallardo like that,' commented Lista, 'unless he's knocked him out and dumped him somewhere.'

'I think two men should go back and scour every nook and corner in that alley,' said Palencia, 'while the rest of us keep in four squads and search every alleyway leading to the two main paths that descend to the Bajondillo. I warn you it's a bit of a maze, but my men know it like the palm of their hand.' The local inspector gave rapid instructions which were heard by Bernal and Navarro over the open radio frequency. 'Comisario? Will you arrange for my *cabo*

173

at the station to send all the mobile units he can muster down to the Paseo Marítimo to cut off the bottom exits of the cliff-paths?'

'We'll do it at once,' said Bernal. 'I'm returning to the Paraíso now.'

By the first glimmer of the false dawn, they had found, amid a pile of refuse behind one of the shops, Ángel Gallardo's haversack with the radio intact and the pistol missing, but of Malinsky and his hostage there was no trace at all. The abductor had not made any attempt to approach his house.

Bernal sat disconsolately in the office drinking black coffee and chain-smoking Káisers. He looked wearily at Navarro. 'Where do we go from here? The general alert we've put out has produced nothing, and the squads must be exhausted by now.'

'We'll search the whole town house by house if necessary, *jefe*.'

Bernal shook his head. 'It would take much too long, and Ángel is in the gravest danger, even if he's not been killed already. Malinsky must have got his pistol and threatened him with it.' Bernal got up with sudden decision. 'Call my driver and get Varga. I want to take a look at Malinsky's house.'

The sturdy dark-haired technician came into the office with his excited assistant. 'We've got a lead on the *etarras*, Chief. I noticed that the powerful Czech transceiver you picked up at Cabo Pino had a wide band of frequencies, five of which were pre-set on the memory device. My assistant has spent the entire night listening in on all five, and he's spotted a regular call-sign exactly on the hour on one of the bands. We haven't dared send any reply of course, because we don't know the codes.'

'How can this help us, Varga?'

'I've requested two RDF vans to comb the coast from Fuengirola to the south-west as far as Nerja to the north-east, and they're gradually narrowing the range. The problem is

that they can only fix a direction on a short burst of trans-
mission at hourly intervals.'

'Let me know at once if they can pinpoint the source of
the transmissions, won't you? In the meantime, I want you
to accompany me to the suspect Malinsky's house.'

When they reached the Camino de Marcelo it was 6.10 a.m.
As the police car screamed to a halt outside the old two-storey
house, the two policemen who had earlier relieved Varga
saluted. The chief technician produced his *ganzúa* or skel-
eton key and soon had the front door open. Bernal told the
driver to wait with the policemen and ordered them to use
their guns to arrest the suspect if he appeared.

The furnishings of the house were curious: heavy country-
style furniture stood in both the downstairs rooms, but the
bedrooms were amazingly luxurious, the principal one having
apricot-silk hangings and bedspread.

'Does Malinsky own this house, Varga?'

'No, sir. He's rented it for six months. I found the contract
in the desk.'

As soon as he had made a general recce of all the rooms,
Bernal began to search the living-room more methodically,
leaving Varga upstairs to look for clothing or luggage that
could have belonged to the six missing youths. After an
hour's perusal of the papers in the old roll-top desk, Bernal
noticed the edge of a flat piece of plastic under the bottom centre drawer. Using his penknife, he gently drew it out.
He saw it was a key with a large green-and-white tag
engraved with the number 14 in black. Of course! This
was the room key which Keller had never been able to
return to the Lido Apartments. Bernal knew he had his
piece of evidence now. He shouted up to Varga: 'Found
anything?'

'No, Chief. Nothing I can be sure of.'

'Come on down. I want you to fingerprint a key-tag.'
Bernal held it suspended on the knife-blade. 'With luck you'll
find Malinsky's dabs superimposed on those of the missing
German youth Keller.'

When he got back to the Hotel Paraíso, Bernal asked anxiously for the latest news.

'There's nothing, Chief, except that the foreign press, beginning with *Paris-Presse*, *La Stampa*, the *Sun* and *Der Telegraaf*, have plastered our missing youths all over their front pages, alongside sensational accounts of the Costa bombs. One of the English papers even makes a joke about them: "HOLIDAY COST-A BOMB." '

Bernal sighed. 'I thought it would come to this. Ask Madrid for permission to seize all the foreign newspapers carrying the story that are on sale on our patch. We don't want the suspect warned. Then call Palencia in and ask him to arrange for all the other officers to be relieved, with help from the neighbouring forces if necessary.' Bernal slapped a thin book on to the table. 'Here's Malinsky's passport. Get the photo reproduced and sent to all units. The Montevideo police should tell us via Interpol if he's got form there.'

At 7.45 a.m. Bernal decided to call Consuelo.

'Where've you been all night, Luchi?'

'The op was a disaster. It went totally wrong. I'll have to stay here until Gallardo's been found.'

'Not that nice young *madrileño*?'

'Afraid so. I was using him as bait. How are things there?'

'We haven't had much sleep here since the explosion. The children are over-excited. When will you be back?'

'Expect me when you see me.'

As the sun rose and lit up the bay, heralding another scorching August day, Bernal went once more to the detailed wall-plan of Torremolinos and stared at it as though trying to divine how Malinsky had evaded his pursuers, encumbered as he was by a hostage trained in self-defence techniques. Either he must have forced Ángel at gunpoint to accompany him, or he had rendered him unconscious and carried him. Since the criminal hadn't made for his own house, he must have a hideout somewhere in the Bajondillo not far below the upper

176

town, Bernal reasoned. That was where the house-to-house search must begin. What could be the significance of the wild-cats on the rooftops opposite the Casa España? They must have played some part in the weird activities of this man with a very diseased mind.

Bernal slumped into a deep armchair and closed his eyes. Slowly he went over in his mind all the events of the previous evening, especially what had happened on the rooftop when Varga obtained the sample of meat. Then Bernal sat up with a jerk.

'Paco? Did you take tape-recordings of all the radio messages from last night's operations?'

'Yes, Chief. Three spools were running.' Navarro pointed to the bank of recording machines.

'No, I mean the operation in the Bajondillo, when Lista and Miranda first tailed Malinsky back to his house.'

'Yes, I've got those, too, on another spool.'

'Play it back for me, would you?'

Bernal sat with his eyes shut, listening to the whole series of recorded messages. When he'd heard them all, he said: 'Now rewind and let me manage the machine. Show me how to stop it when I want to.'

'There's a pause lever on the side, Chief.'

'Have you got a stopwatch?'

'I'll just have a look in the forensic kit. There should be one.'

Bernal now sat in front of the machine, with notepad and pen. He timed each of the messages sent by Elena, Lista, Miranda and Varga, and noted the length of the intervals between them. Then he returned to the wall-plan.

'There's a discrepancy of at least four minutes, Paco,' he exclaimed.

'What do you mean, Chief?'

'From the moment when Malinsky was reported as having left the roof and Varga began to fish for the meat, Lista made off from the T-junction by the Britannia to pick up the trail along the transverse lane. Now, if Malinsky simply shinned down the drainpipe of one of these cottages' – Bernal pointed to the spot on the map – 'why did it take him four or five minutes longer than it did Lista to reach the bottom lane? The only conclusion is that he stopped off somewhere. I'm going to take a look.'

'We'd better take a strong force, Chief.'

'But it must stay out of sight. I'll simply take a morning stroll along the Bajondillo.'

'Please take your pistol and a small transceiver, then,' begged Navarro, knowing how careless Bernal usually was of his own safety, as though he believed he was immune from ordinary dangers.

'You must stay here and co-ordinate everything. Get Palencia to rustle up a squad of armed plain-clothes men.'

At 8.15 a.m. Superintendent Bernal descended in the hotel lift to the garage and emerged on to the Bajondillo. He realised he had been foolish not to visit the place on foot sooner. He usually solved his cases by getting to know every centimetre of the *locus delicti*, as though the spirit of places talked to him of what had occurred there. Now he stopped to sniff at the smells like an old mastiff on the trail of intruders.

He walked up the irritatingly widely spaced steps as far as the Casa España and peered over the railings at the roof-tiles, where a colony of famished multicoloured cats were prowling threateningly, unaware that they had been deprived of their late-night meal by his orders to Varga. Bernal now took out the stopwatch and checked how long it took him from the corner of the Britannia along the lane that ulti-mately debouched near La Roca. Three minutes. Now, as he turned upwards into what seemed to be a dead-end cluster of decaying cottages, his senses became hyperactive. Some-where here must lie the criminal's hideout. He checked his position in relation to the high roof of the Casa España, just visible beyond the lower roofs of the cottages, from which some of the wild-cats peered down at him, hissing angrily.

Bernal started the stopwatch again and stopped it when he reached the corner of the lower lane. Two minutes. Even allowing for Malinsky's climb down the drainpipe in the dark, it could hardly have been more than three or four. Yet the criminal had actually taken seven or eight minutes – double the time. Why? Bernal lit a Káiser and slowly turned back into the group of old cottages under the high cliff. Behind them he could see a long row of tall battered doors that enclosed what seemed to be sheds cut out of the cliff. He began to stroll casually towards them.

Malinsky was slumped exhausted in a moth–eaten armchair with the pistol resting on his knee, while three of his pet cats rubbed their mangy fur against his trousers. He could hear occasional loud groans from the next room, which caused him to gloat inwardly. He would show the bastards that they couldn't make a fool of him! This one he was reserving for later, when he had got his strength back. His back still ached from that terribly burdened descent he had made in the early hours.

All at once he was roused by the sound of footsteps out-side. He rushed to the battened door and squinted through the cracks in its planks, with his finger on the trigger of the gun. At once he relaxed; it was just a stout old gentleman, unseasonably dressed in a grey suit and tie, apparently taking his morning constitutional.

As the stooped figure got closer, Malinsky could see the narrow clipped moustache and noticed the remarkable resemblance to the late General Franco. Something in the stern features disturbed him, and he stood alert, ready to fire if the old man should attempt to enter. Surely he was too old to be one of those who had been searching the area during the night?

The old man passed within half a metre of where he was standing, and Malinsky held his breath. Another loud groan came from the other room. He peered out to see if the old man had heard, but he didn't stop or give any other sign of having noticed it. The Uruguayan left the doorway and went in to gag his prisoner more tightly as the cats squealed loudly with anticipation.

*   *   *

Bernal, whose hearing was remarkable for his age, had caught the human groan and the squeals of the cats; he also sensed very strongly the proximity of an evil mind. He turned back down the hill, past the sleeping cottages, and turned into the lower lane where Palencia and the squad of plain-clothes men were waiting.

'Keep your men out of sight, Palencia. I'm sure he's in that row of sheds; I think I heard Gallardo groaning. We must do nothing to provoke Malinsky into killing his hostage. What are those sheds used for?'

'When I was a child the fishermen used them to hang up the fish for drying and for smoking. You can see the old chimneys rising above the rock from the kippering-sheds.'

'It's a difficult place to raid.' Bernal took a sudden decision. 'Let's call in the chief of the GEOs from Fuengirola and we'll look at the detailed maps with him to see if his men could approach unobserved.'

'Do you think Malinsky's got more arms than just Gallardo's pistol?'

'There's no way of telling, but one thing's clear: we mustn't risk Gallardo's life.'

By the late morning, the GEO unit had arrived and its chief was closeted with Palencia and Bernal to plan the operation. At 12.45 p.m. they visited the Casa España to examine possible approaches from Elena's balcony, causing Albert and Anna even greater astonishment at the Spanish girl's apparently shameless orgies.

'He couldn't have chosen a better place, Comisario,' commented the GEO chief. 'It looks as though we'll have to make a frontal assault after dark.'

'What about those old chimneys above the sheds?' asked Bernal. 'Couldn't you lower some men on ropes and drop some stun-grenades and gas-canisters down those?'

The GEO chief scanned the cliff-face with his prismatics. 'It might just be possible. I'd like to take a closer look from the roof of that pub opposite.'

Despite Palencia's protestations, Bernal insisted on accompanying the GEO chief up to the attic of the Red Lion. The young officer climbed out on to the roof as Varga had done the previous evening and crawled towards the edge that overlooked the group of cottages. A sudden shot rang out and caused the chief to duck behind a chimney as a flying broken tile narrowly missed Bernal's head.

'Get down! He's firing at us!'

Bernal was shaken. 'That's a very bad sign. He'll be expecting a raid now.'

'Can we afford to wait until the early hours of tomorrow morning?' asked the GEO chief.

Bernal considered the matter. 'We really can't take any more risks. I think we should attack as soon as it's dark.'

With Palencia and Navarro's assistance, the plan was worked out to the last detail. Six GEOs would descend on ropes to the narrow roof of the sheds and drop gas-canisters down the chimneys, while the main force would attack from the rooftops to each side, using stun-grenades as they forced the doors. Bernal insisted on watching the operation with Elena from her balcony in the Casa España.

As soon as darkness came, the GEOs took up their positions and the street-lights in that quarter were extinguished and the narrow streets cordoned off. As dusk fell Bernal noticed a faint light appear in Malinsky's hideout and assumed it was from an oil-lamp. When the crowds in the lane outside thinned as dinner-time approached, Bernal judged that the right moment – if there was to be one – had arrived. Malinsky must be very tired by now, and was probably hungry as well. The long hours of waiting must have taken their toll of his nerves. Yet he had a very powerful physique and it was essential to neutralise him right at the start of the raid.

Bernal gave the signal on his transceiver, and watched as the six GEOs began abseiling down the cliff-face at an impressive rate, as the rooftops on each side of the sheds became black with their fellow-commandos. All of a sudden it sounded as though a major war had broken out, with bright flashes and loud explosions, and clouds of yellow smoke rising. Through his night-glasses, Bernal could see the main force break down the doors and enter the sheds. It was all over in a few minutes, and he could see the tall figure of Malinsky, struggling and yelling maniacally, with his arms firmly pinioned, being taken by the burly GEOs to the *lechera* or police van parked in the lane.

'Let's get over there,' he said to Elena, who stood breathless by his side. 'We must find out if Ángel's OK.'

They ran down the wide steps and round the corner to the police vehicles.

'Have you found Gallardo?' he asked Palencia urgently.

'He's still inside with the others. They're cutting him down now. I've sent for more ambulances.' Palencia laid a hand on Elena's arm. 'I shouldn't go in there if I were you, Inspectora.'

Cut down? More ambulances? Palencia's words rang ominously in Bernal's ears as he began to run up the slope towards the sheds. Inside, the GEOs were rigging up arc-lamps which cast a lurid glare on the almost unbelievable scene.

Beyond the mean room where Malinsky had been over-whelmed, there lay a series of bays where in earlier times the fish had been cut and stretched open and then strung up to dry or be cured. The original wires and pulleys were still installed under the smoke-blackened beams.

In the first bay the GEOs had cut down Ángel Gallardo from where he had been strung up and were lowering him gently on to a stretcher. He was unconscious, with a large and ugly contusion on his right temple and blood caked on his face and neck. Bernal felt his pulse and found it beating strongly.

'This is my inspector,' he said to the GEO chief.

'We'll get him straight to hospital in Málaga, Comisario. He's concussed, but he's got good colour.'

As he walked along the row of bays, utterly nauseated by the overpowering stench, Bernal was shaken to see six naked bodies hanging from the rafters, their arms and legs fixed to the suspended wires. They showed signs of having been savagely tortured. The GEOs were climbing quickly up to bring them down.

'These must be the six missing youths,' Bernal said. 'Are they dead?'

'Two of them are in a very bad way, but they're all breathing.'

With growing anger, Bernal walked slowly past the mutilated bodies and green emaciated faces. What unspeakable practices had Malinsky engaged in during all the days that these poor creatures had been imprisoned? The strong oblique lighting made the scene Dantesque, resembling some of the paintings he had seen in the Prado; it was straight out of Hieronymus Bosch.

'Get these lads to hospital immediately and see what can be done to save them.'

Bernal hoped that the Penal Code would provide for penalties sufficiently severe to match these crimes, but he expected that Malinsky's lawyer would almost certainly plead insanity on his client's behalf. Well, he, Bernal, would interrogate him first and judge for himself.

He rejoined Palencia as the six youths were taken on stretchers out to the ambulances. The attendants had started treating them by inserting tubes into the veins of their wrists for saline and glucose drip-feeds.

'Malinsky has been taken to Málaga gaol,' said the local inspector, 'and Inspector Gallardo's been rushed to the military hospital. Inspectora Fernández insisted on accompanying him.'

'They'd all better be taken there. We'll need statements from those that survive for the *denuncias*.'

When Bernal returned to the Hotel Paraíso, Navarro showed him a telex message from Interpol:

HECTOR MALINSKY AGED 41 WANTED BY URUGUAY
POLICE FOR CRIMES IN CONNECTION WITH YOUTH

183

MISSION IN MONTEVIDEO STOP. OFFENCES INCLUDE
ABDUCTION ILLEGAL IMPRISONMENT ASSAULT AND
GRIEVOUS BODILY HARM TO 3 ADOLESCENT MALES
STOP. SUSPECT CONSIDERED DANGEROUS PSYCHO-
PATH STOP. MESSAGE ENDS.

'They can say that again!' exclaimed Bernal. 'We may
yet have to prefer charges of murder. Two of these youths –
presumably the ones he abducted first of all here – are in a
very bad state. The tortures he performed are horrific, Paco,
including attempted mutilation.'

'What about Ángel?' asked Navarro anxiously.

'Malinsky obviously hadn't had time to get to work on
him. It's just as well we moved in when we did.'

'What injuries has Ángel got?'

'A savage blow on the head, probably from when he was
knocked unconscious last night. I'll go and visit him first
thing in the morning before I start Malinsky's interrogation.'
Bernal lit a Káiser. 'I'm off to Cabo Pino now. Let me know
at once if there's any news during the night.'

'Shall I inform Madrid, Chief?'

Bernal pondered. 'No, I don't think we should. Remember, they tried to pull us off this case. Let Palencia report it
to his Chief of Police in Málaga and get him to inform the
various consulates. The families of the missing youths will be
distraught by now.'

Just as Navarro was ringing for Bernal's car, Varga rushed
into the room.

'The detector-vans have pinpointed the source of the terrorists' radio messages, Chief. It's at Tivoli World, the funfair
complex at Arroyo de la Miel.'

'Bang go my hopes of a rest! You'd better recall the Civil
Guard and the GEOs, Paco, while I confer with Zurdo, since
the place lies between our respective patches. I'll also inform
Madrid.'

When Bernal and Varga reached the enormous funfair
and playground complex high above the coastal road, they

184

realised that, even with the portable RDF sets Varga and his assistant had brought, the task of finding the *etarras'* accomplices was going to be a very difficult one, not least because of the danger to the thousands of families enjoying the evening out amid the flamenco *tablaos*, roundabouts, bars and restaurants. Bernal noticed large posters announcing a performance that night at 10 by Rocío Jurado, the popular singer, in the main open amphitheatre.

'We shan't be able to mount a siege operation here, Zurdo,' Bernal commented to his colleague when they met in the manager's office. 'There'd be a panic among the crowd.'

'If Varga and his experts can pinpoint the radio source exactly at the next transmission-time, which should be at nine p.m., Chief, we could clear that area and go in with a small force of GEOs.'

They smoked and watched the clock anxiously as 9 p.m. approached. There was a long delay, and then Varga came in.

'The messages are coming from the amphitheatre, Chief, from the area at the back of the stage.'

'Should I cancel the performance?' asked the general manager in alarm. 'The tiers are all full and the band is tuning up.'

'No, that would be worse than waiting until it's over,' said Bernal, 'though then we run the risk of the terrorists slipping away in the crowd. We mustn't show that there are any security measures being taken. Zurdo, you direct the Civil Guard and the GEOs to take up unobtrusive positions near the amphitheatre, while Varga and I pay a visit to Señorita Jurado. She must be warned about the danger, and decide if she wants to go on with the concert.'

Bernal and Varga found the famous singer already dressed in a silver sequined *traje de cola* – one of those tight-fitting flamenco dresses with a train – accompanied by her little daughter, who was also dressed in Andalusian style, with a mother-of-pearl *peineta* pinned in her swept-up hair. After a brief conversation out of the child's hearing, they had agreed on a plan of action.

When the singer went on to the delighted cheers of the packed auditorium, Bernal and Varga set about searching

185

the entire backstage area. Beyond the star's dressing-room they found a locked door, and they asked the stage manager where it led.

'Down to the scenery store, Comisario. We haven't used any this season yet. I'll get the keys.'

When he returned, Bernal tried the key in the lock. It wouldn't turn. 'You'd better have a go, Varga.'

'Hadn't we better call some of the GEOs in first, Chief? This may be the terrorists' hideout.'

Bernal rang Zurdo at the general manager's office and instructed him to bring a group of commandos to the back of the amphitheatre. Soon Varga had forced the lock, but they found that something heavy had been placed against the door on the inside. As the platoon of GEOs were secretly admitted to the backstage area, Rocío Jurado returned flushed with the success of her opening numbers to change into a red flamenco dress.

'You don't have to go on with it, you know,' Bernal said quietly. 'But, if you do, we'll try to keep the operation confined to the storage room.'

'Of course I'll go on! The audience is fantastic!'

'Then, take your little girl out with you. She'll be safer than in here. And sing your loudest songs, to cover any noise we have to make.'

By now Zurdo, with the manager's help, had located the main scenery entrance behind the auditorium, and he and Bernal synchronised watches to begin the assault on the underground store from both entrances at the same time. Bernal and Varga watched anxiously as the GEOs prepared to batter down whatever the obstruction was behind the door, and then the signal was given.

As the band gave full vent to one of Rocío Jurado's hit numbers, the GEOs went into action, using tear-gas and stun-grenades. From the stop of the stairs that led to the scenery store, Bernal could see some yellow flashes of small-arms fire, then there was a sudden silence. Soon a man and a woman, spluttering from the gas, were led up in handcuffs to where he waited. He looked at their

186

sullen faces with a mixture of curiosity and pity: what a horrific – and, for him, incomprehensible – fanaticism it was that drove them to put so many innocent lives at risk.

'Take them to your station at Fuengirola, Zurdo. There's no reason why you shouldn't keep taking the credit for all this.'

'But that's not fair, Chief. It was Varga's assistant who made it possible to find them.'

'Never mind. Mention him in your report to Madrid. Now let's see what arms they had stored down here.'

Varga led Bernal down to the cavernous depth under the stage, whence they could hear the final overwhelming applause for the great artiste. Clearly nothing had been noticed by her adoring public.

In the still partly gas-filled cellar, where Bernal was handed a mask by one of the GEOs, they discovered the radio transmitter and a large quantity of bomb-making equipment, as well as a pair of grenade-throwers.

'Get all this stuff taken to safety, Varga. If it had all gone up, thousands would have been killed in that amphitheatre. Then I'll go back and charge the male *etarra* with the murder of Palencia's plain-clothes man, Antonio García. I'll want you to make saliva-tests, of course, to check on that cigarette-butt I found in the sand.'

'But what makes you think it was him, Chief?'

'Didn't you notice? He was wearing a signet-ring with a diamond set in an opal on the little finger of his left hand. That exactly corresponds to Peláez' description of the tiny wound on García's neck. I'm certain this was the terrorist who killed him with a commando chop on the beach at Torremolinos when he caught the pair of them digging a hole to plant a bomb.'

When Consuelo saw Bernal's pale and tired face, she nevertheless guessed from his relaxed greeting that the case was over.

'I'll make you some supper, Luchi. We've had ours.'

'I think I just want to sleep the clock round, Chelo. I've got long interrogations to do tomorrow.'

'Have something very light, then,' she coaxed, 'and then we'll go to bed.'

'Get me a beer while you're preparing it. I'm as parched as a camel arriving at an oasis.'

The phone rang peremptorily at 7.30 a.m., and Consuelo snatched at it before it woke Luis up.

'Superintendent Bernal, please,' said Navarro.

'Oh, can't it wait?' she groaned. 'He's very tired.'

'It's very urgent, señora.'

She turned and saw that Luis was sitting on the edge of the bed lighting a cigarette, despite all her efforts to stop him smoking before breakfast. He coughed with the tight and shallow cough of a life-long smoker, and took the receiver from her.

'Paco? What's up?'

'The warders have just found Malinsky hanging from the window-bars of his cell.'

'That was very careless of them. Is he dead?'

'They've tried the kiss of life, but it's no go.'

Bernal was philosophical about it. Was it his job to prevent people from judging and sentencing themselves?

'Now we'll never know what made him do such things, Paco.'

Elena Fernández had kept vigil all night by Ángel Gallardo's bedside. The doctor had told her to keep talking gently to him to pull him out of his comatose state. His vital signs were strong, and it was hoped he'd make a complete recovery.

As the hours passed she became almost mesmerised by the regular bleeping of the electro-cardiograph monitor, and she got over her shyness at holding hands with and talking to a person who was completely unconscious.

She examined his face critically: a good bone structure; the profile was really quite handsome, even Classical, she considered, with the long nose on the same plane as the straight brow, just like those of a warrior on a Grecian vase. The cheekbones were high, the flat ears sensuously lobed, the lips medium-full and well bowed, and the teeth regular and gleaming white.

She sighed as she wondered why she could never fall in love with a handsome man, despite all Ángel's exaggerated efforts to woo her during the five years they had worked together. But she had seen at once that those efforts were simply the Pavlovian manifestation of his *machismo*; she guessed that he was really quite insecure, perhaps unable to love any one woman for long.

Elena suddenly became aware that the fingers of the hand she was stroking were caressing her left breast. My God! He was at it even when unconscious. She leant back sharply and dropped his hand.

'Don't be like that, Elena. I thought you meant it for real this time.' He opened his eyes and gave her a broad wink, followed by a lascivious smile.

'Thank God you're all right. Have you got any pain?'

'Only an outsize headache. What happened to that bastard who strung me up?'

'He hanged himself in gaol during the night, Ángel. Paco's just told me when he rang to ask how you are.'

'What about those other poor kids?'

'Two are in intensive care, but the other four have recovered consciousness at least, including our friend Jimmy, but they've got serious injuries. It's a miracle that any of them survived, especially the two who'd been there for over a month.'

'I managed to talk to some of them when Malinsky was out of the room. He used to let them down one by one twice a day to let them eat some dry bread and raw offal and have a drink of water. I heard from the others that the German and the English youths had attacked him a few nights ago when he was incautious enough to let them loose at the same time.

I gather they put up quite a fight until he succeeded in over-powering them. Since then he hadn't fed them.'

'He was an absolute monster, Ángel. What kind of madness is it that makes people flip like that?'

'He was a very dangerous psychopath. He intended to start on me next, but I knew I'd be OK when I glimpsed the Chief prowling about outside during the morning.'

'He recognised your groans.' She helped him to a drink of water, and then asked: 'One thing still puzzles me, Ángel. Anna, the proprietress of the Casa España, told me that Paulette went back to Marseilles yesterday evening, although she was still in shock. Who was it who attempted to rape her? Can it have been the Angel of Torremolinos? It doesn't seem to fit in with his known proclivities, does it?'

'You mean he was probably coming after me or Jimmy and got into the wrong bedroom? No, it wasn't him.'

'Then, who was it?'

'Call yourself a detective! It was easy to guess who. You yourself said it had to be an inside job, so to speak.'

'Surely it wasn't Albert the proprietor? Old goat that he is?'

'Of course not, silly. Why would Paulette have taken refuge with him and his wife if he'd been the rapist? The French girl knew damn well who it was and she may have invited him in out of curiosity at the start, until he tried to perform perverted acts on her.'

'I'm stumped.'

'If you had deigned to join the queue for the bath-house the next evening, you'd have spotted the culprit at once. Remember Paulette had scrapings of human skin under her fingernails.'

'Don't tell me. It was the curly-headed Moroccan.'

'You've got it in three.'

'Why didn't you arrest him?'

'I put it to Paulette, but she absolutely refused to prefer charges. She said it had been so awful an experience that she could never tell anyone about it, certainly not the judge of instruction.'

'He must have been really something,' sighed Elena, with a mock-dreamy expression on her face.

He dug her in the ribs. 'You'd have a safer time with me, you know.'

'I think it's time I went and comforted poor Jimmy,' she said brightly. 'There's clearly nothing wrong with you.'

'You watch out for that red-haired Irish bull, if he's still in one piece.'